The Algebra of Snow

a novella by

Ginger Moran

MINT HILL BOOKS
MAIN STREET RAG PUBLISHING COMPANY
CHARLOTTE, NORTH CAROLINA

Cover art: Photograph courtesy of iStockPhoto.com,
    design by Chuck Moran
Author photo by: Kromatic Photography

The short story from which this novella is derived was
published in *Feminist Studies*.

Library of Congress Control Number: 2012935039

ISBN: 978-1-59948-360-3

Produced in the United States of America

Main Street Rag
PO Box 690100
Charlotte, NC 28227
www.MainStreetRag.com

To all my parents:
Charles & Fermine Moran,
Mary & Jim Robison,
and Peter Sheras

Contents

The Farm

Nothing could ever be too safe. The woman knew she was silly about it sometimes. A person with a more practical turn of mind would laugh. But she had yet to make herself into a practical person, so she applauded the brick patio between the rest of the Virginia farmhouse and its kitchen. The old house at the foot of the Blue Ridge was wooden and in the kitchen was a big wood-burning cookstove, a Mephistophelean combination without the buffer. She enjoyed the word "Mephistophelean" when she came up with it.

The woman sat on the plastic-cushioned kitchen chair she'd brought out. Snapping beans her husband had harvested that morning and would expect for lunch when he came up from the field, temporarily contented, she watched the little girl play with a saucepan and spoon at the edge of the bricks.

She pinched the end of a green bean with her thumbnail, snapped the body of the bean in thirds, and dropped the pieces in the heavy ceramic bowl on her lap. For now she was not even anxious over crazed rustics with sawed-off shotguns, cows with anthrax, or wolves. Glad for little safeties like the patio, she dropped her recognition of them into the silence of the country like stones in a wall against her future fear.

She was not so afraid for herself as for her three-year-old daughter.

The child had abandoned herself to an elaborate fantasy game with the saucepan and spoon. Several of her favorite imaginary playmates were at her dinner table. She was conversing and laughing with them as she served the food from the saucepan. Occasionally, her invisible companions got out of hand and she sometimes argued with them or hit them with the spoon. But she had her mother's timidity. Even the reprimands were quiet.

The large man was most often a problem. Today he was making a pig of himself, as usual. He often had to be scolded and frequently sent to his room. He was never good about that. He whimpered and begged to come back. Sometimes she gave in and let him sit at the table again, but her real feeling was, if you're going to make a pig of yourself, you'd better be ready to face the consequences.

That was one of the few things she didn't see just the way her mother did. When her mother played the eating game with the girl, she would talk her daughter into letting the fat man back.

The little boy was almost always well-behaved. Sometimes the girl had trouble keeping up a conversation with him. It wasn't rudeness, really, on his part. He was just daydreaming of somewhere else, of other things.

When the girl was tired of scolding the fat man or trying to get the boy's attention, she just sat back and listened to the Pearl Lady. The lady had lived everywhere and told stories about her life in a big city where she walked a Boston terrier with rhinestones on his collar. When her mother played the game, she supplied new stories for the Pearl Lady.

But even the lady could get dull, as she was doing then. The little girl put down the saucepan and spoon and went to see what her mother was doing.

The woman smiled at the child. The girl stuck her hand in the bowl and pulled out a bean section.

"No, baby, it's not cooked yet. Put it back," the woman said.

Mother and daughter understood each other. The girl fingered the piece once more, rubbing her index finger against the grain of the bean. It stuck for a second to her skin, released itself, and fell into the bowl.

"All done," the woman said. She stood up with the bowl in her hands. "You can stay out here on the bricks, but don't go off them. Daddy hasn't mown the field up here yet." She pointed to the tall grass just beyond the bricks.

The girl looked out into the field. When the grass was short it was her favorite place to play. It was bordered on the far side by a low stone wall. Her mother let her play there without supervision because she could not get over the wall and onto the road.

The woman went inside. The girl returned to the edge of the bricks. She banged around the inside of the pan a few times with the spoon.

There was danger in the field, she knew. Once her father had carried her on his shoulders down a dog trail through the brambles and poison ivy to look at a thick black snake sunning itself on the stone wall.

But the cornflowers growing as high as herself were the color of her eyes. She touched her eye experimentally, drooping the lid so her finger didn't go in. She remembered the color from the mirror.

From the open kitchen window the woman watched the girl lift her finger to her eye. She did not call out when the girl stood up and stepped off the bricks. The woman was, for the moment, more curious than afraid, and once she'd begun to suppress her fear, she found it easier to continue. Her daughter was smart enough to understand why she was banned from the field.

Just before the girl disappeared into the tall grass she turned to look toward the kitchen. The look was enough to keep the mother quiet even then. It was not a look of mischief or of defiance but one of regret.

Chapter One:

Labor Day

Now it's my turn to tell you a story, Ma. This one starts ordinarily enough, with two women at the grocery store.

"If a third of your life is spent asleep, what fraction is spent at the grocery store?" I ask Maria, my Stop 'n' Shop partner.

She looks a little puzzled, but these are the sort of mathematics I have become absorbed with at the end of the summer. I persist.

"How much time does an ordinary woman spend shopping? What if she hates to shop? Or, the alternative case, she coupons? By what percentage is the time increased if she has, say, one child? By how much is it decreased if she dies young?"

"We don't fit the test case," Maria, a practical sort, says. She considers the refrigerator case, then leans on her cart handle and looks at me. "We are vacationers at the end of summer in the Adirondacks, buying enough for a last supper without getting anything that might be left over. We are childless. We are already past the time one might be thought to die young. If we died now, we would die in our maturity, or early middle age."

She takes a stick of lightly salted butter rather than the whole box.

"I give up on the problem," I say. "Domestic life has variables the most advanced notation can't express." I follow her down an aisle.

Maria hands me a box of Gaines Burger.

"You can't just take one or two pouches out of the box, can you?" she says.

"I guess this is as good a time as any." I drop the box in and push the cart nonchalantly up the aisle toward cleansers. "I'm not leaving tomorrow."

Maria stays in dog food for a moment, comes down the aisle after me, puts a hand around my elbow, stops me and the cart.

"So you're leaving later in the week?" Maria says.

"Later in the month. Like the end of it."

Maria studies me. She is a small-boned woman, a little shorter than I, dark haired and dark eyed. She has vivid coloring in her face and has on a red shirt and bright blue cropped jacket. I am blue eyed and blonde, taller, paler, and wearing a white sweater with a gray-blue snowflake design across the shoulders. The Southern European and the Northern. It is one of the anomalies of this time in my life that I have befriended someone as quickly and deeply as I have Maria this summer. Grateful for the concern in her black eyes, I would like to slide into them as into a warm lake at night. But some other part of me would be more comfortable with something icier, more distant. I start thinking in numbers again, abstracting myself by habit out of the situation.

"Sweetie, I'm a little worried. Do you know what you're getting into?"

"Yes, I believe I do. I'm cooking dinner for you and Leo."

"Leo can't make it. He's getting the car serviced tonight. Everyone's leaving tomorrow. Except you. Do you know how cold it gets up here?"

"I've been coming to Saranac ever since I was a kid, Maria. And it's only one month: September. I only signed the lease for one more month."

"So, okay, Amelia. Okay." She puts a can of Bon Ami in the child seat. "It can frost even in September," she says. "You wouldn't want to be stranded without cleaning supplies."

We laugh, the laughter of women who keep clean houses, knowing full well it is intellectually and socially frivolous. We know dust returns eternally.

We drive out of town and up the mountain, stop by Maria's, a redwood cabin with a jacuzzi in the back yard. I pull the Saab in behind Leo and Maria's Bronco. Leo is attaching the luggage rack to the roof. I honk. Leo waves to us and stops working. He helps Maria extricate the bag she filled for their trip home. She stretches up to catch the kiss he leans across the bag to give.

"Amelia, how are you keeping?"

He doesn't mean it only as a propriety toward his wife's girlfriend. Leo and I have liked each other from the start. We are both dwellers in the ivory tower, eggheads. Leo teaches law at Rhode Island; I teach mathematics at Stony Brook.

Everyone who vacations at Saranac wears the proper mail-order clothes, but there is something about Leo and me that makes us stand out from the practicing lawyers and CPA's, marks us as academics. Our eyes slide off to the side when someone begins to discuss the legal ins and outs of his contract and the exciting economic potential of his Keogh. We have been friends all summer.

"*Algebrais Universalis* still isn't getting anything out of me," I say, "but the garden grows."

"You're missing out on stuffed acorn squash," Maria says.

"Damn," Leo says.

Leo is of the thin, grey type who does actually like vegetable dishes and will probably inherit the earth. I think about my absent bear husband who would have found acorn squash pathological, immoral, a crime against the human physique.

"Need any help getting ready to go?" Leo says.

"No," Maria says. "She doesn't. She isn't leaving."

He looks puzzled but gives up on the problem quickly, a male trait I admire and rely on.

Maria and I get back in my car.

"He looks like a plaid squirrel."

"What?"

"Getting ready for winter," I say. It would be hopeless if I had to say what was funny about putting "plaid" and "squirrel" together.

"Oh. Did you get pignoles?"

There is a physical sensation in the back of my neck, a tightening between vertebrae, that is the feeling of missing the two people I've ever known who would have gotten the joke and improved on it.

As Maria and I go higher up the mountain and take a few turns, we leave behind most of the cabins. Up here, houses are rough-hewn and lack amenities.

When we jounce down the road to my cabin, you can tell we're in the sticks. Right from the start, the cabin looks peculiar; it has two front doors. The realtor told me it had once been a two-room tavern. That still doesn't account for the two doors unless lumberjacks of old thought two would be handy if a bear came through one. Now, one opens into the living room, one into my bedroom. Maybe the doors satisfy my urge to escape. Just like in one of my few real memories of you, I sleep always with one leg outside the covers. Under the roof is another, unfinished story. Tacked onto the back is a kitchen and next to it, completing the rectangle, what was once a patio has been enclosed and is now a dining room with a surprise brick floor.

A deck has recently been built onto the kitchen-living room side of the house. It juts bravely into the oaks and sycamores that take over where my yard leaves off. Maria and I sit there after we've done the required things in the kitchen.

Maria breathes. "Air smells like sex."

"What do you suppose is so sexy about rotting leaves? The Celts used to start courting at this time of year, when they came back from the summer fields. I know because I married one." This time she twists a smile to me, enjoying the tiny wryness with me.

We already look out of place sitting in the lounge chairs on the deck that is too summery, mistakenly sociable, as the oaks go up in flames among the pines around it. At Labor Day in the Adirondacks, summer is already over.

"Summer is a touch and go affair here, don't you think?" Maria says.

"To a Southerner it doesn't count. Never gets steamy in the day and the nights get cold in July."

My golden retriever comes out of the woods and stands next to Maria, good-naturedly waiting for a pat on the head. He looks a little puzzled when Maria lifts her hand to fiddle with her chunky gold earring. I snap my fingers and George moves to stand next to me.

"Did you tell Donovan?" Maria says.

"Why would he care? He has missed the finer points of our marriage for at least a year now, even when we were still in the same house. Subtleties like my staying here another month aren't going to have much impact."

"I don't know, Amelia. Maybe you aren't giving him enough credit."

"Divorce is hell," I say. I instantly feel bad. I have trivialized everything, not least Maria's sympathy. I wonder if Donovan doesn't have a point about my bitchiness. I drink the rest of my gin.

I stand quietly in the middle of my garden. Maria is inside, doing something in the kitchen or maybe calling Leo. I am supposed to be picking salad vegetables for dinner and I will do that in just a minute. Right now I'm looking. Donovan had a garden at our house. He built raised beds and filled them with peat moss and topsoil, mixing in a small proportion of the sand that made up the rest of the yard. Up here I don't have to raise the beds. The soil itself is hundreds of years' worth of leaf mold and pine bark. Donovan is a flower man; I'm growing vegetables. The growing season is infinitesimal here and I have had to do some thorough calculating to get in long-term crops like the acorn squash that is baking in the oven. Even tomatoes were a little tricky. Right now I'm thrilled to see the pumpkins ballooning among their vines, bright orange against the black soil. I stand there among them, hunched over the heavy square low-ball glass still in my hand like some drunk haggard scarecrow dressed by Lands' End. I put the glass down outside the border of dwarf French marigolds and herbs and begin to cut greens with a knife.

Maria and I are in the kitchen with both the dogs. Galen, the border collie, has streaked in through the deck door and drunk loudly from the stoneware water bowl. Now she shepherds Maria to and from the sink as Maria makes the salad. I'm at the stove, adding to the stuffing for the squash. I have to shove George out of the way to check on the squash's progress in the oven.

"When can you visit? Christmas?"

"I'll probably go home then," I say. Maria looks up quickly. "It's been years since I spent Christmas in Virginia. My father is in his seventies." Maria goes back to her salad.

"I was worried for a minute," she says. "I'm not sure what you mean by home right now, but I guess you don't mean you're staying up here till then." She spreads radish slices over the top of the salad. "You know, we haven't talked much about our parents. My family is still intact in Ohio. I didn't even know where your father lives."

"Virginia. Home to presidents," I say. I sprinkle romano cheese over the acorns and close the door on them. "He's a judge there. I don't really mean to make everything I say sound flip."

Maria tosses in a cherry tomato. "I know. Where does your mother live?"

"The graveyard." This one has gotten to Maria. "Sorry. She died when I was six years old. If you go through elementary school with a dead mother, you get a little calloused."

"You haven't had it easy," Maria says.

"My dad is a very gentle man. We lived in a wonderful old house, with my grandmother most of my life. She had terrifically kind housekeepers. It wasn't so bad."

"Still," Maria says.

I'm watching Maria who is herself terrifically kind and who has become more important to me this summer than any woman since high school. She has understood both the general grinding one goes through in divorce and what particulars I had to offer. I wonder what it will be like to do without the kind of accompanied space she has afforded me this summer. I wonder if I'll survive.

"The trouble is I don't know if I live up to your level of sympathy. Divorce is so commonplace. Even when it started happening to me, I was more surprised Donovan and I had managed to stay together four years."

Maria is watching me. Her hands are wet still from the salad and they hang down in front of her, slick, going on forty, the left one weighed down with thick, faceted, old-fashioned wedding rings. She lets me go on now.

"We were like the black and white Scottie dog magnets I played with with my mother as a child. If you turn them one way, they rush together. But if you turn them tail to tail, they bounce apart."

Maria's eyes fill up. She steps over to me. I am pressed into the corner between the stove and the wall with the little window that used to look onto the patio and now looks into the dining room. Maria puts her arms around me.

I feel the muscle and bones and warmth of her arms and can smell the perfume still lightly contained in the crevice at the base of her throat. She is a little shorter, her breasts press a little below mine. I believe I could stand here a long time, filling up my woman quotient. And yet I step back first, twisting sideways, as a rush of cool October-smelling air blows in the deck door and oak leaves rustle against the screen.

After Maria leaves to go home to Leo, I clean up the kitchen and put the last few groceries away. I had planned to spend the evening working on the manuscript I think will guarantee me tenure, but I find myself distracted. I think about Maria and what it was like when I was in boarding school: the easy, unbidden company of women. I miss it, although I have not thought about those women for some time.

At the boarding schools the other girls had acquired math anxiety with the onset of puberty. I never did get anxious over math; I was more anxious over my period not starting. By the time it did, at sixteen, I was through Trig, inexorably on my trek across Calculus.

In grad school at Columbia, I got more passionate about algebra. It is the most refined form of what mathematics is: a system for moving symbols across a page. I finished my Ph.D. in five years, did two years post-doc and teaching at Columbia, then was hired at Stony Brook, where I have been for three years. I was considered a golden girl and given tenure credit for my two post-doc years and then I raised my capital by publishing my dissertation. I was on accelerated tenure track, up for it next year, when I stalled out and stopped being able to finish articles. My gilding was enough—and a woman in mathematics that close to succeeding rare enough—to convince the department to give me a year off from teaching to try to get back on track. When I came up here, I meant to get several articles finished to prove I could, but I got increasingly distracted as the summer went on.

If, instead of being my mother, you were someone I'd just met, I would say my mother died when I was six. My grandmother died when I was fifteen. My father is a judge in Virginia. My husband is a ne'er do well.

But why, now, does this summary strike me as the moment in the funeral where the sermon has been said and the mourners go outside into winter air to get in cars to drive to the interment?

And, by the way, is anything other than a corpse "interred"? Is this a situation-specific word?

To recur to the subject: I mean to spend the year working at home, on the beach, and really intend, as I said to Maria, to stay here in the mountains only for the month of September.

But it's true, I admit in the quiet of Maria's absence, I am falling in love with the idiosyncrasies of this house. The house has history. It was not always what it was when I first saw it, a picture far in the back of the *Adirondack Life* ads. Mrs. Greene, my friendly realtor, was dismayed, I could tell, that someone like me, so clearly accustomed to the modern (my Saab suggests all things clean and Scandinavian) wanted to rent something so odd and used. And, for the first part of the summer, I had wondered too. But now I think I see my point.

Take, if you will, the kitchen. It was added on the back of the tavern and its roof slopes downward sharply toward the ground like a summer camp lean-to. People who are even just a little taller than I cannot stand up near the acute angle of the ceiling. But I can stand back there, sheltered under the ceiling, and look out the playhouse-sized window which opens upward on hinges.

I stand there now, with Maria gone, and watch my dogs play in the leaves of the forest that stretches forever behind my cabin. They are on the other side of the rickety split-rail fence, near the stream. Galen crouches with her forepaws out and her head down. She yips at George who stands in the middle of a circle she begins to describe around him — she the pencil, he the point. She picks up a stick and waves it in the air. George accepts the invitation on those terms and chases her, reaching out with his huge gold paw when she stops to tease him again. Finally, she lags just slightly behind in her withdrawal, he lunges, and they race off into the woods, each holding an end of the stick in the gloaming.

It's getting cool, dark. I take out the piece of wood that is propping the window open and hook it. Pouring another glass of wine from the bottle Maria and I bought for dinner, I look around the kitchen once more, checking surfaces to be sure they're clean — the white enameled tin-topped table that serves as a counter, the wooden table I eat breakfast on: farmhouse furniture. There are no stray dishes that have materialized in the sink since Maria and I stood side by side there after dinner, she washing and I drying with the furnished, threadbare but still mighty white linen tea towel.

The sink itself is long and shallow. The drain is flat, not a little basket. It would be a good sink to bathe a baby in, much better than the one at my house in Stony Brook, which is double stainless steel with a garbage disposal to suck everything down.

Donovan is trying to sell my sink, along with the rest of the house. I doubt that he will sell any of it, to tell you the truth. Even though the realtor is handling it, Donovan would have to find it convenient to let prospective buyers in, which would mean he would have to clean it and himself up somewhat, and I think this is beyond him now. I'll try to sell it when I go back. Since Maria left, I have begun to wonder, really, when that might be.

In the meantime, I am in the living room of the cabin and have my hand already on the phone to call Donovan before I stop. It has been a while since it was sincerely my business how he is and he will find some way to find fault with the inquiry now: I don't really mean it/Why didn't I ask before?

I am sitting on the sofa with the white phone on my knees. I have put my glass of white zinfandel next to the big yellow lamp on the old, rough oak cabinet next to the sofa. I put my hands against my belly, making a shield between me and the phone that is still on my knees. I just sit.

My house is a log cabin. No one has ever sheetrocked, so it is log inside too and thus always dark. The living room is the one most occupied by people who were here before. Hordes, it feels like, just outside my direct line of sight. I'm not talking about ghosts. I'm talking about a random-width heart of pine floor that is worn around the grain. Between the planks is dust going back two hundred years. Or at least this is possible, if not entirely probable.

What has caught my attention, distracted me from calling Donovan is the window behind the desk, in the right-hand wall from where I sit on the sofa. Someone got a wild hair to modernize—maybe the same one who closed in the dining room and made the deck—and got so far as to put in a picture window which marks the place as a summer cabin. It is absurd, grotesque, a third aperture in the face of the house. No real Adirondackian would have that much glass exposed on the north side.

The sun has gone down and I can see myself clearly in the window, my face projected on the dark screen by the yellow lamp, lit, next to me. I can see the glass of wine and the sofa.

What stops me—it seems so frivolous, I almost hesitate to mention it—is the decor. But this is just the sort of thing you'd be interested in, Ma. The sofa is an old overstuffed, dingey white one. At the beginning of the summer I covered it with a peach colored sheet bundled together and tied at the corners. It's the most homemade of covers. No one has accused me yet of being good at home decorating, or, for that matter, homemaking.

But for some reason the soft couch and the fact that the sheet, the wine, and my face are exactly the same shade of peach champagne bring me a sense of peace like flying along feet up on a sunset cloud.

There is no need for me to take action. I don't need to do anything for my father (in his quietude since your death, I don't know he needed anything from me anyway); nor from Donovan (I'm just as useless to him, despite his clamor); nor for my job (how badly can algebra need someone?).

This is the first time in my adult life I can remember feeling peace, this cozy enfoldment. I'm staying.

Maria and Leo say goodbye the next day over steaming cups of coffee I've brought to their driveway. It is the day before Labor Day. Maria's black eyes look at me through the car window with a concern I now don't feel for myself, as if I should feel guilty for not being more anxious. We haven't much to say. I lift my coffee cup to her, and she lifts hers to me. For each of us, there is some question about who is offering the stirrup cup to whom. They go off in mist and dust, crunching leaves.

Most of the other summer inhabitants leave the same day. They take the bright colors and shouting children and parties, leaving behind the natives and me: glittering water withdrawing from creviced rocks. It becomes cool enough to wear a coat. On Labor Day the tips of the lettuce leaves in my garden are curled by the hot breath of frost. I pick the last green tomatoes from the emaciated vines and put them in a brown bag on top of the refrigerator to ripen. The gray herbs—thyme, marjoram, and lavender—have finally come into their own; they are heartier, as if at home in the moors, while the gentle Southern mint is devastated. Sometime during the day it occurs to me that classes have started and

I think about calling the department just because I feel the tug of the academic tide despite being on leave. Or at least I might work on the manuscript the *Journal of Algebra* has already expressed an interest in. But I am digging potatoes that are finally harvest size. Potatoes' chaotic method of reproduction—ten large spuds out of one eye, only two tiny, unbelievably sweet potatoes out of another eye planted at exactly the same time—is interesting me far more than the ultimately calculable kernel of -1.

The week after Labor Day slides by. My cabin is above where even the natives cluster. I rarely sight another person. When I go to town early the next week the post office clerk seems a little surprised to see me; she identifies me as someone who, earlier, had chatted, but we both now honor a distance. She gives me the package that wouldn't fit in my mailbox, and leaves it at that.

Maria has sent me a care package. Included are trail mix and a bottle of my perfume, items so clearly required for survival in extreme circumstances, tears surge into my eyes as if I've been unexpectedly kissed by an angel. She has also sent pictures from the summer that in my mind is already "last."

There are some pictures of the Fourth of July picnic Maria and I gave together at my house. When I glance at them in the car there is something odd. When I get back to the cabin I take them out on the deck to study them in the light. I sit in the wooden armchair, with coat and glasses on, and try to make out what is spooky. Galen comes to assist.

Take this picture of me and Leo. We were on the deck and there are people all around us. Everyone is dressed in white. Leo has on a white knit shirt and cotton shorts. I'm wearing my white Mexican dress with red flowers embroidered on the yoke. I have white huaraches on. I'm holding a gin and tonic in one hand and am gesturing upwards through the trees with the other. I look perfectly serious, but Leo is laughing, so presumably I'm saying something amusing.

I may be making wondering comments about God or the weather, given my gesture.

One picture is of people playing volleyball in the small open space between the garden and the trees. It's a cramped but enthusiastic game. Roger is spiking the ball. He has driven it down so hard you can't even see a white blur in the picture.

This is probably a pretty good sign in one's lawyer, of which Roger is mine. He is also a friend from childhood, his father and Father having gone to law school together. His family and Father and I vacationed together in the Adirondacks.

Roger was a good enough summer companion. He was a quiet and well-behaved boy, the boy qualification being an important one to me. I became accustomed to the company of men early and preferred their obviousness. Roger and I taught each other how to sail a Sunfish through trial and error and many turtlings of the little boat. We laughed every time we dumped it, the amusement, even relief, of children who are ordinarily so competent, so successful at what they do.

Roger turned out to be a good-looking boy: reddish-brown hair, craggy features suggestive of Hyannis Port, a tan and fit body. But our relationship stayed what it always was: the easy companionship of two well-bred, essentially nice people.

I lost track of Roger when we were in college. I heard from my father of a move to New York, a marriage and then I believe a divorce. I had meantime fallen in love with Donovan and there never was space enough in Donovan's and my world for anyone else and frequently not enough for breath. When it came to the divorce, I called Roger. He found out I was spending the summer back in the mountains and decided to come up, too. He'd already been up twice before the Fourth of July. He stayed with me. At the time I blanked out the fact that he's very attractive.

But I can see in the picture that, in shorts and shirt that look like uptown bvd's, Roger is immensely attractive. Still the reddish-brown hair, the crags to his face, the All-American body. If my black-haired, blue-eyed bear-built husband had been there, he would have been on the deck arguing with the men and flirting with the women in a charmingly caddish way. As a matter of fact, he might as well have been there, for all the attention I paid Roger. But, looking at the picture again, I can easily see that, of the two men, most women would say Roger is the more desirable.

And now that I'm looking at him, I can see in the pictures a look on his face that says he was interested in me as more than a friend this summer. We did have history, and Roger had never remarried. The day after this picnic we'd taken the Catamaran out on the lake and visited spots around the perimeter that we'd explored as children. I remember coming back to the cabin to a sun-glutted dinner of party leftovers and then a long game of gin rummy on the deck. I remember Roger's hand reaching past the citronella candle as I was putting the cards back in the pack, and I remember standing up just then to say I was beat.

I had begun to understand then that I was up to something. After my quiet childhood it had been surprisingly easy to become a social being; everyone wanted in on the self-sufficiency I wear as a cloak. It was no different at Saranac that summer. But I repaid my social debts with the Fourth of July picnic and, though I wasn't entirely clear about it then, I was finished with most people. I remember leaving Roger on the deck that night, his hand quickly drawn back, and going to lie on my narrow bed.

Roger was a man my father would approve of. But even nice men spike the ball. Is it a flaw in my moral makeup to prefer a man who is more straightforwardly abusive on the sidelines?

I do remember this about that night: on my bed on the Fourth of July I gave myself to the pleasure of listening without distraction to the night noises. I started down the cool steps of sleep. I thought immediate thoughts—the distance covered that day in the boat, what there was for breakfast. Then there were more removed ones—the way Donovan holds a tiller, negligently; the sight of my dogs running through a field in the sun somewhere. The field was full of a carnival and I bought a ticket to the Ferris wheel from a dwarf in a Navy uniform. My heart did one of those galvanic contractions and I woke up just enough to know I'd been falling asleep. I dropped myself into the dream with an absolute satisfaction, cleaner than the ambiguous fulfillment of lying in bed with someone else. It was a subtle, exquisite self-abandonment.

Looking at Roger in the photograph, I realize we've had only technical conversations over the phone since then. I hope he doesn't feel rejected and imagine himself in more sympathy with Donovan. What Donovan and I feel for each other can't legitimately carry a name as tidy as "rejection."

In any case, I can remember the solitary pleasure of that night perfectly, but I can't remember what was going on in these photographs. They're perfectly good Canon 35 mm photos, but they ought to be fifties, garish technicolor; they feel at least thirty years remote to me, not the six weeks vintage they actually are. Maria and Leo have only been gone a week, but the week's quiet transported me from shorts to jeans, has laid down a boundary between me and this other time. I might as well be looking at a picture from childhood, where you see the image and somewhere in your mind it resonates, but it is so muffled you can hardly believe you ever wore those clothes, had that expression on your face, knew those people. Do you know what I mean, Ma?

CHAPTER TWO:

Halloween

T he thing is, you have to hit the middle of the wedge with the middle of the sledge hammer. If you do, the wood shatters perfectly, popping in a wooden way as if it had always wanted to give up the bond between grains and is just plain grateful you gave it the opportunity.

If there were a man here, I'd let him do this because I'm not very good at it. Of what use is eye/hand coordination in a mathematician? So, more often than not, I pound the stump next to the target log, leaving the wedge untouched and waiting. Or I hit the corner of the wedge, knocking it out of the log it was meant to split. I put the hammer down, put the wedge back in, pick up the hammer again, replant my boots, lift, aim, swing.

When I have a disreputable pile of irregularly split logs and some kindling, Galen carries a piece inside for me and I pile the rest in a canvas carrier and haul it inside. There is no need for a fire right now, in the middle of an extraordinarily sunny October day, so Galen and I leave our burdens and go out the side door to the garden.

"One holiday about which I'm ambivalent," I tell Galen, "is Halloween. Know what I mean?"

It goes without saying she does, at least the general parameters. Nevertheless, I explain. "At Thanksgiving the only pressure on you is to eat. It's pretty harmless, as holidays go. Christmas, on the other hand, is tricky: unspeakable desires are raised and then merely irritated by the application of inadequate material assuagement. But Halloween: I've had good ones and bad ones."

Galen is in complete agreement. We have gone down the deck steps together and are standing outside what is left of the garden. The heads of the marigolds in the border have long since been blackened and hung by frost; even most of the herbs are gone. There are some baby pumpkins that never got very big and now never will. Their vines are shriveled, gray-green.

Under Galen's supervision, I collect the pumpkinettes and line them along the deck rail beside others I have already picked. None is carved, but all of them have personalities. Some are tall and thin, a little concave along the sides, very British. Others are squat and some are slumped over, prematurely inclining in the direction in which they will all eventually collapse. I won't put candles in them. Without faces, it would be silly.

I won't leave the front light on tonight either. No children will trick or treat my house. I'm pretty far out from the village, and the few houses on my road are deserted summer residences. Besides, I think I may be getting a reputation.

Maybe the villagers are beginning to associate me with the sidh who must live up here if they live anywhere in New York. But then maybe the villagers don't know what sidh are.

Donovan knows. He says them "sheathe"; they are supernatural beings that simmer in the earth and lakes and trees until Halloween where in so many cultures they effervesce over the membrane that separates them from humans and seethe among the living. Ma, you are sensitive to this sort of thing, inclined toward the Celtic. I believe you would have been interested.

Father, you know—Puritan from way back—would think of it all as nonserious, silly, okay as entertainment but beyond that faintly odorous, as is anything that confuses the clear distinction between election and damnation.

As for my reputation up here I don't really know or care what the people who live here year-round think. But I did get an alarmed call from Maria the first week in October. She had been calling the house in Stony Brook and got nothing—no Donovan, no machine, no me. So she tried what she thought would be a disconnected number. I hadn't actually had a conversation with anyone for quite a while. It may have been a week since I'd heard a voice; I'd taken to using the money machine at the bank and listening to classical music. When she called I got the feeling there were lags when I was supposed to respond, like I'd forgotten the rules of grammar and syntax and logic and was waiting for someone to fill me in.

"So just one more month, Amelia?" Maria said.

"You know, Maria, I think I've forgotten how to conduct a conversation."

"I'm coming back up there."

"No, no, no, no. It's my work. It started going really well in the middle of September."

"The article for the *Journal of Algebra*?" Maria is suspicious.

"No, a different one. I'd done notes for it a long time ago, back when I was post-doc, before I met Donovan. I didn't know how to pull it together then, but the work I've been doing since helps. I've gone pretty far with it in the last couple weeks and I think I've got something. I don't know yet whether the solution will be trivial or not."

"Trivial?" Maria said.

"Doesn't actually need proof, axiomatic, obvious."

The blizzard of mathematics numbed her concern. And I was telling the truth. The problem I had made notes for five years ago happened to be in with the papers I brought to work on and I'd gotten very excited about it, seeing maybe now I had the wherewithal to approach it. It could be a really good problem, reputation-making, a breakthrough. On the first of October, the idea had carried me through signing another month's lease, though the garden was already blasted and George was occasionally registering a complaint about the cold floor and his aging hips. Galen was satisfied, though. Her coat had come in thick and sleek. She wanted to go out early every morning and stayed out till dinner.

Halfway through October, I could still see the problem spread out on the desk in front of the summer window from where I sat on the couch, phone on my knees, talking to Maria. It had been at least a week since I'd touched the papers and there was a tiny layer of ash on them from the woodstove I lit at night.

So I may have signed the October lease in the name of the problem, but just two weeks later that wasn't my purpose anymore. I wasn't sure what I'd been doing since I abandoned the problem, but I knew Maria's presence would be interruptive if not disastrous to whatever it was.

"I think I'll have it by Halloween," I tell her.

"Okay, Emmy," she says. "I'm trusting you."

Have what?

At Samhain, I still don't know. I return to the deck at the end of October where I am wrapped in my coat in the slatted wooden armchair, blue-jeaned and booted legs hung over an arm of the chair, mind mesmerized by the row of pumpkins. I come back from the memory of the phone conversation with Maria, two weeks old now, as if I've been travelling. I've been doing this a lot lately. Except usually I don't return to the cabin with a specific memory but only with a sense of having been gone.

Does the lack of acuity bother me, you might ask? Not necessarily. It's drastic, and I haven't met a mathematician yet who isn't some sort of extremist. Sometimes we say to ourselves we will stop at some reasonable point, but we hardly ever do. To stop when it is not yet required would seem just plain silly; it would make us crabby; it would be like someone taking away our child before it was grown.

I come out of the meditation with a plan ready-made. I have not been thinking directly about this problem, but of course I have a solution. I go into the house for hat and gloves and car keys but get distracted.

I fetch a black army blanket from the bedroom closet and tie it around my shoulders. I go back out on the deck. Galen is in the yard next to the ruins of the garden. George is with her, having appeared from the forest. I toss the flap of the blanket across the lower half of my face and waggle my fingers at the dogs. Galen comes to sit next to me while George lolls over on his back—it isn't vigorous enough to be called a roll—in a pile of leaves.

Dogs are unbelievably consistent. Of course Galen would instantly recognize and want to ally herself with a witch. And George can always be relied upon to be royally indifferent to my self-amusements.

"So, my girl," I say to Galen, "will Mrs. Greene get it? No, of course you're right. Disguise, to a realtor, is always a little suspect."

I leave the blanket in the bedroom, check to be sure the fire is out in the woodstove, and whistle Galen into the back seat of the Saab. George is sound asleep curled on top of the leaf pile, blending into its golds and browns.

It is a violently beautiful day, warm enough really for me to leave hat and gloves at home and to shuck my coat. I take only a jean jacket and get into the car with Galen. As we pull out of the drive, the cabin sits foursquare, gray-brown in the midst of the flames of the trees. George, sleeping on the pile of leaves to the right of the house, and the log-splitting stump in front are the vertical strokes suggesting the joining of what blaze there still is in the trees with the ground-fire of leaves below.

Despite the warmth, even the tag ends of summer people are gone. As I drive down the rutted stone and dirt road away from my cabin, I check out the other houses, finding them satisfyingly deserted. I am wickedly enjoying the fact that no other non-native is here to receive the shock of this autumnal beauty.

As we bump up onto the paved road and into the clear, I pop in a cd. It is one of Galen's old favorites. As Bob Dylan blows the whistle at the beginning of "Highway 61," she cocks her head over to one side. I can see her in the rear view mirror.

"Want to hear it again?" I ask her. I push the cd button and play the beginning of the song again. She puts her head up as soon as the whistle stops and cocks it, ears forward, as soon as Bob blows again.

Dogs are so satisfying.

"Mrs. Greene," I list for Galen, "then the electric company, gas, phone, grocery store, then home." This plan has sprung full-blown into my mind. Only the execution remains. Relieved of any further need to make decisions, I feel conversational. We drive.

"Can you stand the way we girls have to do all the errands while the boys sleep?"

Galen turns around once and lies down on the back seat. She looks alert, intelligent, and resigned when I glance down between the seats at her face.

"Let's just take off," I suggest to her. I speed up, rushing past the field of cows along the flat road. "Who needs those boys anyway?" I sound excited by this possibility, enthusiastic. Galen sits up, clearly concerned. She nudges my shoulder with her nose. She isn't the sort to whimper.

"Okay, okay," I tell her. I slow down. But I've worked myself up to such a pitch that I'm not sure my disappointment is feigned. "Let me ask you this, as a means of distraction: Why do you suppose these cows are all lying down? In the summer they only do that when it's going to rain. But it doesn't look like rain now." The sun is actually hot through the windshield and I have the window an eighth of the way down. "Do you suppose cow-rules change in winter?"

Galen is magisterially unconcerned about this. I'm not going to get her in a flap again, at least not over cows. We turn into the real estate parking lot.

"Amelia, it's none of my business," Mrs. Greene says, "and it's surely my pleasure to keep the cabin rented, but you do know the snow starts in November? And it isn't just a little dusting. I'd feel irresponsible if I didn't point this out to you."

We are at her desk in the small real estate office, dead now compared to when I first came in May. It is also suffocatingly over-heated. Mrs. Greene is a caricature of motherliness—round, hair gray and tucked in a wonderful, neat bun, frumpy suit. There is no question this is dressing for success in her case; the conviction would rise unbidden in a prospective house-buyer that whatever house she showed would not only be tasteful but also somehow good for you. She has never been crazy about my choice, though.

"Yes," I say, "ma'am," I add inadvertently. I try to recover. "My work is going very well and I don't want to interrupt it for the move right at this moment." This is an explanation that makes no sense to her, I can tell. A cold honeymoon would make sense to her. "And my husband is coming up." This is a desperate lie, but all I want is out. It works.

I sign a lease for November. Mrs. Greene presses a Styrofoam cup of coffee into my hand as I go out the door.

"Keep warm, dear," she says. "I'm so happy for you."

I too am elated as I leave the office. My body, which has begun to feel leaden lately, now feels light, floating buoyantly down the path into the Saab.

"Snow," I say to Galen. She actually had been asleep on the back seat but covers well when I open the door. "The snows start in November. I'm looking forward to multiple school cancellations."

I drive to the electric company singing "la-la-la" and then on to the grocery store. It's vegetable-beef stew for us tonight. I have preserved the peas, carrots, onions and potatoes from my garden. I buy beef, three shoulder bones, milk and a newspaper. I hum through the checking out process. The checker, a much sourer older woman than Mrs. Greene, pretends she doesn't hear me. I smile at her anyway.

As I drive out of town and start up the hill, clouds roll suddenly in on an imperious dark wind. I stop la-la-laing. About half way down my road a little blonde girl, maybe six years old, steps out in the road some distance ahead of me. She is dressed in a fairy costume and, though it is hard for me to imagine where she is coming from or going to, she runs across the road purposefully. Even at this distance, I can see her fairy wings. She doesn't have even a sweater on: it would crush her wings. She is chased across the road by wind and leaves. I am close enough to see her face is pinched with resisting the cold. By cruel, unintentional contrast, her costume floats diaphanously around her. She is gone by the time I get to her section of the road.

We all had stew and the dogs are happily grinding shoulder bones to dust outside. I sit at my desk with a pile of untended business. Donovan sends the bills from Stony Brook without a note. I write a check for the homeowner's insurance and make an entry in my green budget book. Then I open the property tax bill. It's a whopper. I walk around the house a few times, go out on the deck to check the dogs. I try to walk out from under the feeling of oppression finance nights bring on me. For a mathematician, I have a terrible aversion to this practical application of numbers. I remember the late nights my father spent behind the gauze-curtained French doors of his study, paying bills or taxes tirelessly, a wizard. I never saw any ill effects of those long nights. I decide to call him.

"Daddy," I say, "how are you keeping?"

"Amelia," he says, "this is a surprise." He chuckles a little.

All well-born Southern men have choir voices and my father's timbre is one of the best, even if he doesn't say it's a pleasant surprise.

"The years roll on," I say.

"I guess so," my father says.

Not even I am sure what I meant.

"How is Long Island?" he says.

"I'm still in Saranac, as it happens," I say. Silence. I rush into it, arms flailing. "Work was going well and I didn't want to move the whole shebang. I should have two—no, make that ten—articles done by Thanksgiving."

There is a short silence and I will him to ask why I've upped the total so drastically, but he refrains. "What, do you have the computer up there?" he says.

"Computer, microwave, everything." This is a pile of electronic falsehood, but for some reason I think this sort of technological bulkiness is a reason for staying he will understand. As with Mrs. Greene, I see it not as lying but as mercy. "The thing is," I go on, "it's gotten a little hard to make ends meet, keeping two houses going."

"Donovan," he says.

It's just one word, in his most resonant voice, without the inflection of a question or an exclamation. It stops me cold. My father doesn't know what to make of my profession, but he knows what to do with my husband: disapprove. He doesn't hate him. He is merely disappointed in my choice, and maybe slightly surprised at himself for raising a daughter who could have committed such a lapse.

"What do you think of the divorce, Daddy?"

"Well, Amelia, I'm sure you're doing what you think best. I trust your judgment."

I had been getting ready to ask him for a loan, but for no reason, anyone—nevermind my father—having trust in my judgment is amusing. I move the phone to my chest and laugh.

". . . flowers for your mother," he is saying when I put the phone back to my ear. I haven't adjusted to listening totally yet. ". . . contribution?" I think he says.

"Sure," I say smoothly, like a Virginian, despite not knowing what he is talking about. "I'll send it right away."

"Keep it rolling," he says.

I light candles in every room of the house and turn off all the lamps. Having done that, I don't know what comes next. I sit on the edge of my bed, an old-fashioned pallet mattress lifted up high on a rustic four-poster with heavy carved oak acorns at each corner. I push off the heels of my shoes and let them drop from my toes to the floor. I take off my rag pullover and the navy blue sweater that used to be Father's. I take off my flannel shirt and my light thermal t-shirt. I take off my jeans and rag socks and underpants. I make a nest of the bedclothes and pillows and lie in it for a while, until, through the window, I see the moon is quite close to full. That gets me out of the nest. I open the door. Although the final October air ought to be much too cold on my bare skin, I hold my arms up and shape them exactly around what will soon be the Hunter's moon. Satisfied by this embrace, I lie back down on the bed, on top of the covers. I have left the door open and I wait for deer against the moon.

Grandmother would know what to do. She was the strong figure in the family. We lived with Grandmother all my life, except for the two years at the farm and the short time in the new house just before you died. Even the new house was next door to Grandmother's. At our new house, when Grandmother came for the midday meal, she twisted your ironed curtains up away from the windows so that the view to the outdoors wasn't obstructed. Gardens were preferable always to the interior and the peopled. My guess is that Father married you to redeem him from the impersonal.

Just like *The Snow Queen* which, when you read it to me, you read with a passion that seemed personal. Did you see the old woman as the heartless Snow Queen, absconding north to her frozen kingdom with the boy, her son, your husband? Did it occur to you after a while that no quantity of your tears could melt the ice chip she'd put in his heart? When love fills a woman's heart, is there any way to understand that some damage is irrevocable? I was your fulfillment more and more as it became apparent that there would be no more children and that Father could never be fully rescued from the snow kingdom.

To you, then, I owed unspeakable loyalty not only because I'd racked your body coming out (both of us on laughing gas, legend has it) but also out of personal choice. But you were eventually not only the weaker one but also the dead one and, along with your life, gave up most of your advantage.

I fell back on Grandmother, although on some level I think I must have understood her form of strength was one of infinite regress. Mother, Father, Grandmother—it was by this triangulation I navigated as a child, even though one angle was haunted.

I get up from the bed and blow out all the candles around the house except for the one I'm carrying. That one I put in the refrigerator and close the door on. I am covered in goose bumps and get instantly back into bed, without waiting to see if the flame goes out.

But it wasn't Grandmother I was looking for; I was looking for Father. And in the dark this is what I find:

My father in three parts: Atticus, Abraham, and Dopey.

Father specialized in civil rights law before he became a judge. As a child I saw him as Atticus Finch in *To Kill a Mockingbird*. He did take me to sit outside restaurants that wouldn't serve black people and we got telephone calls in reference to our racial preference which frightened my mother and caused Grandmother to look disapproving, though whether of the caller or of Father's activities it was hard to tell. But the image of Atticus itself I wasn't entirely responsible for: Father took me to see the movie twice while you were in the hospital. Although a child that age generally easily makes distinctions between celluloid and reality, it gets harder in black and white. Besides, I needed something firm to believe as you rapidly, silently, mysteriously disappeared. I was not allowed to visit you in the hospital.

Father and I did things non-stop those few hospital weeks. By doing we kept the dark out, twirling and twirling to multiply the images of the last few lights. To this day I use this form of grief-resistance: keep things bouncing, no matter what; keep very busy; be polite; don't start talking because it may never stop; for heaven's sake, don't scream. Talk about not stopping! We went to the movies. I remember being taught to waltz, dancing around the kitchen standing on Father's toes. Working puzzles with him and doing word games. His brushing my hair in front of the woodstove.

It was only a great deal later that I understood the worst had happened to me: I had succeeded. You were dead and Father loved me. I had won the Oedipal fight. For about a month. Then he vanished finally and forever into his grief. I think that must have been when I first realized you were gone. I must have looked around pretty wildly for you then. I had loved you extravagantly, as you had taught me to, and then I had loved Father the same way for a while. If he wasn't going to be available, I by golly wanted you back. But of course the only extravagance you were indulging in by then was growing your hair and fingernails luxuriantly in your coffin.

So I had to make do with the image of Atticus. The fact that Father sat down outside restaurants in protest is in itself admirable but does not necessarily guarantee the intense personal commitment to protecting his children Atticus showed. I didn't make this out till much later, when I was away at school.

With apologies to the headmistress, he took me out of my first boarding school because I led a student protest there. It turned out that principles are a good thing, but one wouldn't want one's daughter to have one.

I remember sitting on the edge of my bed then, at my grandmother's house, trying to think of some way I could have reversed what I had done. I tried to take it back. But there was no way I could think of.

In the long run, the murdered turned out to be my opinion of Father. I had to go on, but without my belief in him. At the time it happened, I thought it just changed his image. He turned into Abraham. Only he was an Abraham in the eyes of an unbeliever. His mission in my life was over. Although he stood over me with the knife lifted, he had changed. He could no longer compel, not as father nor as judge. He had changed, but I had not.

I would always be Isaac. I had been raised to be Isaac, the sacrifice. I would always be a slim, naked body on the stone slab, lifted up to test my father's faith. I would always be Isaac the son.

Never a daughter. Never a woman. Never a mother.

Ways in which men turn themselves into cartoons: by betrayal, mostly.

Betrayal of what they pictured themselves as: Father as kind, liberal. But really he was frozen in the tundra of responsibility to a woman whose strength and intelligence were used to spread the hoarfrost.

My father never did marry again. His mother died when I was away at school senior year. He let the last housekeeper go.

Meanwhile, in my mind the Abraham cartoon had changed into Dopey, the Seventh Dwarf. When Father married you, he had just seen the new Disney film—Snow White. When he met you, he stood on Sneezy's shoulders so that he could dance with you, Snow White. And then he could dance with you forever in memory. And there I am, too, dancing behind Dopey, a small blonde shadow, holding his knees. Maybe the blond shadow has the nubs of angel wings, she's so young. She's maybe disappearing back into pre-life: she doesn't have that much to hold her here. She's hanging onto Dopey's skirts for the time being, though, as he dances—hopelessly, on so many counts—with the ghost of Snow White.

I get up, find a candle and a match, get the budget book from the desk, and take it back to bed. I wrap the quilt around my shoulders. On the top line of October, "rent," I start writing, straight across 1 2 3 4 and on into "total." Then from "electric/gas" across.

"Daddy," I write, "why have you asked for this money for Mother's flowers?" Some dark part of my brain has reconstituted the request on the phone my conscious mind heard only imperfectly. "Are you financially strapped?

"What if I wanted to buy her something else? What if I wanted to give her a tiny pink blown-glass box? A piece of watered silk that will run and shrink in the rain, turn pale in the sun on her tombstone? A magazine? A fox-tail tippet?

"And while we're at it," I write across the "miscellaneous" row, "did you love your mother? How do you feel about dying? About the daily passage of time? the cosmic? Do you have faith in God? in your mind?"

I'm into November now, already halfway down the page. My pen is electric, racing across the narrow rows.

"What makes a good life? Is it work or love or family or travel? Is it nature? Is it home? Do you think your parents loved you? Is there an afterlife? Do you care? Is there any personal message in your will?"

I remember that in one of the upstairs room I'd stowed a box of photograph albums I'd taken last time I visited Father. I wonder if there is any information in there, any clues. I drag the quilt upstairs with me, holding it together at my chest with one hand and carrying the candle in the other. I ignore the scrabbling in the roof structure, find the box, and put a crumbling black photograph album under my arm. Downstairs and back in bed, I open it and find, tucked inside the front cover, a packet of letters. The ones in front are airmail blue, with faded brown fountain pen ink, written in my father's handwriting, addressed to his mother in Virginia. The postmarks are from different places in France, dated before my birth. The ones in back are regular white envelopes, addressed to my grandmother at her winter home in Florida address.

I'm not sure I want to know this—as remote as he is, I'd still like to think he didn't have a life before I got there. Nevertheless, this is clearly my next task.

January 17, 1947

Dear Mother,

> *As soon as one pushes off, one longs for the land. I know my "Grand Tour" (if that phrase continues to have any currency in this post-War world) has been postponed long enough and Europe, though devastated, still is the source and repository of the western world's culture. I know I have gone quite long enough without my "Tour," as you have so often pointed out as part of your lifelong effort to urge independence on your children. And yet it was my pleasure to serve you during those difficult war years, and we did send two emissaries in my brothers, who, all praise to God, came back essentially whole.*
>
> *These are the sort of wellings-up one feels on the ocean, although I don't remember them from our other crossing. Perhaps there isn't nearly so much to toss about in a ten year old's mind as in a thirty-four year old's.*
>
> *But I don't mean to be studying nostalgia, although as the ship tosses its way across the Atlantic, I walk the solid*

red clay of Virginia always in my dreams and memory, turning, with you, now to the lavender of the lilac bush, now to the oriental red of the japonica, admiring the fresh blue against dark green gloss in the tradescantia and periwinkle. This is, I see, where this peroration began and is quite a good place to end.

Your loving son,
Edward

I knew my father had taken the usual Grand Tour every young man of his class did, and I knew he had been very attentive to his mother. I had no idea he had such a poetic turn when it came to describing Virginia. The letters are in chronological order. I open the next one.

15 Feb 1947

Dear Mother,

We dock at Le Havre in the morning. I am hoping there will be letters waiting in Paris, as two weeks without communication from my family seems very long indeed. I trust you have been able to finish up your last-minute gardening chores and push off to the Florida cottage. I know what a curse it is to you to be shut up indoors.

I confess I feel some anxiety over having deserted you. I know my bondage to you would be the last thing you desire and yet I understand you have depended on me as your eldest child and son, especially as Father's behavior degenerated into impossibility. As always, I salute you. And I stop right there. You will think the ocean air has made me maudlin. Credit it to the lack of activities on board ship. My regards to brother Morris.

With sincerest affection,
Edward

This new form of extremity interests me—the attachment to his family—but I will lose it if I stop to examine it, so I open another envelope and drive into the night.

8 Mar 1947

Dear Mother,

 I hope you'll forgive the three-week silence. Although I don't remember Paris well from my earlier visit, it seems now like a dog that, still alive, has been beaten and starved. I am staying at the Lyonnais, as you suggested, but I confess the splendidness of its gilded candle sconces, the magnificent old, thick carpets and the velvet fleurs de lis of the wallpaper seem out of keeping with the devastation of the city and its people.

 I make my way to the museums every day and have found satisfaction in hiding out among the antiquities. The Jeu de Paume has held the most charm for me with its Impressionist and post-Impressionist works. I won't go on about these as I know you deplore experimentation in art as much as you do FDR's taking us off the gold standard.

 The cafe is closing and I suppose I have drunk sufficient coffee and smoked assez de Gaulois for one Paris evening, so I will sign off with my usual regards to Morris (you might remind him of the pipe bomb we once constructed to assassinate the cows who affronted us).

Your always loving son,
Edward

I knew about my grandmother's economic conservatism, which went along with a belief in the old social order while fully embracing individualism politically and the romantic style in the garden. But I had never imagined my father smoking. I now can see him clearly in the cafe, the small blue pack next to the tiny white cup. Am I to give credence to his love of the Impressionists too?

6 April

Dear Mother,

 I have been spending some time in the gardens here, taking notes on the design and plantings for you. You would be appalled by the topiary, but there is something nevertheless grand about the will to sculpt and control trees when a civilization has been shocked the way this one has.

You will notice my address has changed. As I continued to live in this city, its devastation became more appalling to me until my guilt sent me running from the Place St. Michel straight to the ninth arrondissement and, me voila, the Joan of Arc Hotel. I don't expect to have mystical visions here; it seems, in fact, very proletarian, clean and serviceable. I expect to be here two more weeks and then will begin my journey south.

Ever your son,
Edward

It is some unspeakable hour of the morning. I begin to doubt the reality of what I'm reading—am I dreaming? But I don't doubt the veracity of what I'm reading, any more than I do the conversations I have with you. The conversations, the letters—both true, all mad imaginings.

1 May

En train (literally)

I have been taking my time on this part of the journey, meandering through the scarred countryside and visiting the homes of artists and the like. There are many splendid homes, of course, but the one that was most affecting, I felt, is Monet's at Giverny. The gardens reminded me very much of yours in their luxuriance of growth and the care that went into their planting. Your sense of color is more delicate than his—there is little white or lavender or plain green to be found at Giverny but instead a madness of red and yellow and purple and flame. I felt very much at home in the midst of all that growth and could almost see you on your camp stool, leaning over to weed a bed of tulips, dressed in your blue denim jumper and cotton shirt, your white hair wisping around your face and your hands, square and useful like mine with good black dirt permanently lodged under every nail and a look of pure, abstracted contentment on your face.

I had a revelation inside the house at Giverney. It is very, very simple—all white with rooms having one dominant color each, yellow or blue, and scrubbed-looking pine furniture. Perhaps when I come home filled with artistic ideas I'll take the project of the interior of our home in hand.

Your son,
Edward

Galen has come and hauled herself up on the bed. The candle next to me is guttering. I find another one, go on. I don't know this man, this son, who has been so transformed by what he saw that he would take on the daunting task of managing his mother.

30 June 1947

Dear Mother,

I cannot go on. That is to say that I can't go on the way I have. For the past two months I have been in the south of France and in the Pyrenees. Not only is the countryside excoriated, so too is the spirit of the people. And the children, oh my God, the children. They are being kept in camps—French children, Spanish, Jewish, even English, who were caught unaware by the war and their parents shoved them out into the countryside to save their lives. Who knows where the parents are? I have been working in the resettlement camp, run by the American Friends Service Committee, for the past month. I find all images of peace and beauty and art and culture completely obliterated by the faces of these starving, abandoned children who even now, two years after the war, live in a camp. I can find no justification for the wrongs they have suffered.

*I will move from here further east soon, going to join a
work camp also run by the Friends in Poland. I will notify
you of where you might reach me.*

*One bright spot has been my introduction to Polly
Collins, a fellow American. She is working with the
children too, also somewhat accidentally. She was
travelling from her point of arrival in Italy to join up
with her sister, a WAC, in Paris and was stunned by the
children as well. She has been working here two months
and now must go on, to my disappointment.*

*Her family is originally Alabamian: Birmingham.
(Do we not have some Birmingham connection? She and
I think there must be one.) She grew up on Long Island.
The Collinses are a good family and you would enjoy
meeting her. She is quite lovely. She isn't very practical.
She is more like one of the flowers in the garden than like
the gardener. The experience here in Spain has been rather
hard on her. She does have esprit, though, and we've
whiled away some evenings with discussions of art or
literature and, more frequently, politics. (I'm afraid I shall
be returning a great deal more political than I departed.)
In any case, Polly will be visiting her brother at school
in Charlottesville and I have recommended she pay you a
call. I'm sure you'll be attracted by her brightness.*

As ever,
Edward

I have few letters to go. I take the quilt around me out to
the kitchen to get a glass of cold water and return to my bed.
I submerge. I won't come up again until this is over.

February 8, 1949

Dearest Mother,
*I feel duty bound, somehow, to try to prepare you for
changes you may see in me. Two years of rebuilding roads*

in Poland tend to change one's perspective. Something of the granite and concrete we work with creeps into the personality, I suppose. As you know from my letters, the work has been hard, the living often very simple and sometimes truly primitive, but the fellowship has been very rich: the Poles themselves are tough, independent people who have recovered from horrors you and I will never experience or even be able to imagine. It is inevitable that one feel humble in their presence.

I also find my erstwhile interest in art for its own sake is completely eradicated. There is, after all, reality. I cannot imagine just what form my work will take upon my return. Art history is out of the question.

I don't quite understand your comment about Polly Collins. I am glad she finally was able to pay a call and I see that you agree that she is quite lovely. This is what I meant by brightness, or at least that is what I recall of her: a nimbus of softness and femininity among those sad children. I know you value a person for his or her intelligence and perhaps that is what you understood as bright. Polly is quite intelligent, I'm sure. I should think you'd have hit it off instantly. As I understand it, she is now thinking of living with her brother in Charlottesville, according to the letter I got from her (in which, incidentally, she praises both your beauty and your wit).

I am looking forward to being home and getting to work on projects around there. I will let you know when the train gets in.

Edward

June 6, 1950

Dear Mother,

You will be delighted, I'm sure, to be the first to know that Polly has accepted my proposal. I count myself among the luckiest of men. I'm sorry you won't be here for the ceremony—it will be small, soon, and in the Chapel—and

I hope the Florida cottage is now in good order. Polly has agreed that living in your house will be the best thing for everyone. She doesn't seem to mind that the work I do—more a social service than a job—has little remuneration. We will be ensconced in the upstairs wing by the time you return.

Your happy son,
Edward

6 Oct 1952

Dearest Mother,

Polly has made you a grandmother! Hallelujah! The child was born at 6:20 PM last evening; she has all the required parts. Polly is well, delighted at this arrival after what seems like a long wait. The house will be ringing with newborn cries when you come from Florida.

Daddy Edward

5 June 1955

Dear Mother,

We have moved to the farm and I have begun preparing to put in a fall crop. Polly is a little anxious over the remoteness—she doesn't have your spirit of adventure—but is heard to be humming as she deciphers the mysteries of the old cookstove. The child seems pleased with the whole idea of the country. Hope the trip to Nova Scotia continues to be interesting.

Your son,
Edward

15 Nov 1958

Dear Mother:

There is very sad news for me and mine. The doctors have found breast cancer in Polly. It is too late to operate. I don't know, really, what to say. Polly is bearing up, although I don't feel I have ever really made her happy.

She was happy enough at first to live in your home, and I know she was thrilled when finally the child came. Then she wanted her own home and I hoped the farm would please her, but that too proved a poor plan. She did think it right that I go to law school. It seems a terrible tragedy that this should happen so soon after we bought our own home. I know you have sometimes thought Polly a poor match for me—flighty. But I know you will be truly aggrieved now. I hate to burden you, but I need your help. Please tie things up in Florida and come back as soon as possible. Some plans must be made for the girl.

Your son always,
Edward

And now, on this bed in the Adirondacks, the bare skin of my arms an alarming shade of blue and having arrived nowhere near morning, I still cannot make out, in the mist and fog and silence of memory, whether it is Atticus I see, into whose lap I would give anything to crawl if only he were the sort of kind man who would shoot a rabid dog to protect his child, and not Abraham—another possibility—who will use his weapon against me. Or if indeed the figure is—do I fear this more?—only Dopey, and we'll whirl around the room one more time, he enchanted, me barely keeping up, laughing, confused, unnoticed.

My father in three parts: Atticus, Abraham, and Dopey. I could weep from the confounding of the parts the letters have caused, but I will not.

CHAPTER THREE:

Thanksgiving

The dogs are thrilled to see me up on All Saints/Day of the Dead, especially George. For him every day means more doggy things to do—another chance at the squirrel (the same one, to his way of thinking, capable of self-multiplication and projection in whatever direction he happens to be looking), another bowl of dog food, more fun with Galen, another possible bone.

To George, time is an endless freight train of present moments: it's always "now," then "now," then another "now." This is true of him; Galen sometimes seems a little haunted.

I give them Milk Bones and a bowl of milk each and take a cup of coffee into the living room. George makes his exit through the kitchen door and vanishes into the dark woods. But this morning I've gotten up too early for Galen's approval. She climbs dainty-pawed onto the peach sofa and goes back to sleep. I chunk logs into woodstove's hot coals and open the cocks as well as the flue. It doesn't have the appeal of a fireplace, even with the door open, but its thunderous rumble when the logs catch is satisfying, subterrestial.

When I stand and look out a less hearty face appears in the window than the peach one at the beginning of the fall.

The hair has gone a little lank, though it has acquired an almost hairdresser-induced frosted look as more threads of silver-white shoot through it. The cheeks are hollow. Along with the leafmold, the more starved trees outside, the snow I think I can see suggesting itself to the hills in the distance, there is something fitting about this.

I sit at my desk and concentrate on the problem I am transforming now. It is more a game than something I will use in a paper, more the sort of problem Donovan would have brought to me when we met.

The way a problem is laid out at first always daunts me. You might think such a blizzard of numbers and letters and functions would steer one away from a career in mathematics. But it isn't that way. At least it isn't after I've oriented myself, centered myself above this particular plethora of hieroglyphics and remember it comes down little by little, piece by piece, a deciphering on the left, another on the far right, a reduction of the equation to its next, more concentrated form.

Galen jerks her head up from her paws hanging over the edge of the sofa. I look up from the problem. She looks at me sitting in a pool of lamplight with pencil poised, then she looks away, out the big window behind me where it is still not dawn. She just gazes. After a while, she gets up and goes to the kitchen. I listen to her lap water, her tags ringing against the ceramic bowl. She comes back in the living room, gets back up on the sofa, turns around once and settles back down again with a whump, a collapse—a little bit resented, a little relieved—of her body and with it the structure of whatever vision she'd been having.

I still can't find the transform by integration as t approaches infinity and negative infinity.

If you think understanding about Father helps, you're a little naive, a little too hopeful, Ma. There is a flaw in the psychotherapeutic model and one very similar in the rescue-through-artistic-expression concept: there are some things over which one does not get. I can talk this over with Freud himself and it will not change the fact of the axe cut in this tree. I can sing arias I have written myself and they will come straight out of that cut, but never will the sap glaze it over. Don't even consider the bark's growing back—much as you'd like to.

I cannot see Father as anything but a cartoon—fading into the walnut paneling of his study, his face pouched with dispassion, whose cruelty toward me wasn't even intended, I existed so little to him.

And what did this ultimately mean to me? That I forgive too easily, don't expect much from men. That I must always have distance—how else can one make a cartoon? And what is the price? I am forever attached to the casually contradictory: distance, bad boys, independence, flirtations, and manly behavior—mind and discipline. I am stuck with the cartoons, although they can never mean anything good to me.

Dating was like renting cartoons. This probably sounds cruel to you. It might have been. Men told me I was heartless. I had trouble understanding what people meant by the word "heart." I dated one man for three years in college, then walked out on him two weeks before our wedding. Then I lived with a man first year in graduate school who could compete with my father in both looks and kindness. I couldn't understand why any more than he could, but I walked as soon as we'd picked out a sapphire engagement ring.

It was for their own good, I came to understand later. They both went on to marry women who had more than a vestigial heart. The second one I stayed friends with even after his marriage. Several years into the marriage but before I'd met Donovan, I had dinner with him and his wife. When she took his plate off the table, she leaned over and kissed his elbow. It came naturally to her.

So it was good for them that I'd left, but I've never had altruism as one of my defining characteristics. What was in it for me? When I saw that genuine, loving kiss, it hit me hard. Not because I wanted him, but because I wanted that. I watched like the kid outside the candy store, only the window glass against which my face was pressed was colder, more tensile because I had been inside once, had walked out of my own volition, had locked the door behind me and dropped the key down the storm drain, choosing the sharp edge of pure if lonely peace over the soft contour of unremarkable companionship.

The problem is small, personal. It is sad—but also quite common, and not nearly so bad as other fates. And one must learn at some point irrevocability applies to lost principles, lost hearts, lost lives, and lost children. They cannot be called back from the dead, especially if one begins to doubt they ever had any vitality beyond one's enormous desire for them to live.

It's not as if I'm going to die from it: this isn't a ballad. I was going to go on doing what needed to be done, contributing what I could, withholding as much poison as possible. You weren't like this, Ma, but can you understand what I'm driving at anyway?

There are people who remember no flame. There are people who never doubt it. There are people who are haunted by the memory of its warmth and brightness, who believe they see it again in the peripheral vision and would give anything to pass through it again, would gladly trade places with Joan of Arc. But the flame isn't there. And luckily at that point I betrayed the wish only by little flick of my head, had barely swung my hair.

I rest my head on my hands on my desk and drop into sleep. I am at the farm we lived on when I was very young. There are two of me in the dream, one—instead of the girl I actually was—was a boy about two years old. The current me is standing on a hill watching. On the other hill my father is working in a field. Between us is a slope-sided ravine, into which nestled the farmhouse. The child has escaped you,

Ma, and has cleared one retaining wall. He's headed for the one near the road, completely serious in corduroy overalls, tow-headed. My father puts down his hoe. He scans the road from his height to see if there are any cars coming. He moves down the hill, but his pace is clearly not meant to save the boy before he gets to the road. Ma, you might suppress that panic once in a lifetime; to Father, it was a habit. There are no cars coming. The boy goes over the wall and across the road as if this is his job. He's going as purposefully as a good executive down the creek bank when I start to run. Father runs too.

Is one of us going to get there in time, before he drowns? If so, which one? How swift is the water? How deep is the stream? How fast are we going? How far away are we? How long is the creek bank and what is the baby's speed? Does he walk, crawl, or fall?

Factor in exactly how determined he is to drown. Finally, determine whether or not I am real enough in the dream to save him if I do get there.

I wake up. Galen is asleep. Does she remember the puppy farm? I don't think so. She isn't, after all, a cartoon. I need to be careful about turning everything into one. One formula, no matter how quadratically gorgeous, does not fit every set of circumstances.

I reach toward her without touching her. Her twitching paws, muffled yips, tilting eyebrows calm me, bring me back to where everything is as safe as it can be.

As November progresses I spend more time with Galen than with George. Galen was Donovan's puppy when I met him. We joked about the mismatches we'd made with our pets. I'd had George for years and we both are on the blonde scale, though George is much more a strawberry shade. And that's about it for similarities. He is a chunky dog and I am a small-boned woman. He's a happy, athletic, masculine dog. My mind is masculine, but it isn't macho: muscular, not monumental; not a football player, no lineman, or even a quarterback—maybe a wrestler, a middle-weight.

Donovan is dark-haired and white-skinned—colored like his border collie—but that's it for resemblance there too. Galen is dainty and fast. He is big—a solid, square body that inclines toward fat, as any good Irishman's will. When he took me in his arms at twilight it was like going into fur in a dark cave: warm and living and safe. He lumbers like a black bear when he walks.

Once, at the end, I saw him lumbering down the street by the Seven-Eleven as if he'd escaped from the zoo. He didn't seem to understand the concept of the sidewalk and so was shuffling through the leaves in the gutter. It must have been a bad drunk. I was driving and didn't stop. By then it was way too late.

He let me bring Galen up to the mountains. I think even he knew by then that he might forget to feed her for unmeasured periods of time. Though she may be haunted, she knows I belong to her as much as Donovan ever did, in a steadier if less fun way.

As November progresses Galen and I accompany each other through days beginning to look remarkably similar. They have the simplicity and clarity of convent life. We are up early, go to the bathroom, make coffee, release George, work a little while at something, clean up the kitchen, make the bed, put away any clothes, coats, and books that have gotten littered around the trajectory of the previous day. We might work some more through the late morning, or do some household project like cleaning the refrigerator. Though none leaves more than a confectioner's sugar dusting yet, the snows come more steadily, and the house acquires a reflective, glittering pristineness inside.

We discuss Donovan, not always verbally. It seems natural; she has been with him longer than I. And, with the kind of unboundaried childhood I'd had, it seems natural too, now that I think of it, that I would fall only for a man who had the strength to create himself in my presence, even if it meant cutting into the limitless space of my self, even if it hurt.

I met Donovan when he appeared in one of the classes I taught when I was post-doc at Columbia. He had grown up in Boston, the middle of five boys in an Irish family. In big Irish Catholic families the boys have possible roles to choose from: One is married to his job as to the priesthood. One is so ruined by drink and drugs he is a suicide-to-be. And one is marginally irresponsible. His bad habits constantly show the promise that they might be redeemed by his being an artist. That was Donovan. He had a great talent for memorizing poetry and wanted to write it. Although his working-class roots made jest of his ambitions, his Irishness did not.

Don't get me wrong. I'm not speaking ill of this system. Given the lack of possibilities in my Episcopalian childhood, where the only choice was to be a sort of lank-haired generic girl in golf skirt and espadrilles or muscle-tight, reptile-shirted frat boy, Donovan's family seemed rich to me, having a multiplicity of cultural codes to choose from. Even the tragic ones enchanted me.

That was before I really got to know his family, especially the ways in which Donovan was going to incarnate their heartaches. His father was a drunk. His mother wept every day and looked for weak ways to enslave her sons.

But when Donovan first came to my History of Mathematics night class, I thought of him simply as a fairly intelligent cab driver. I had the cab driver part right, anyway. He'd been driving one for five years, frequently driving it around to bars, until he drove up to Columbia one night and registered for classes.

But he was more than fairly intelligent. He was mercurial, moving faster and having more brilliance than anyone I'd ever known. He came up with original solutions and conjectures that had no practical application but make up the sort of play that is to a mathematician what truffles are to the epicure. He wanted to know what about the Renaissance epistemology gave rise to algebra and the connections among calculus, Newton, and Kepler. Why all at once? Was there a causal connection? Or was there simply a thought around? What is so threatening about mathematics that the Roman soldiers killed Archimedes while he was figuring out grains of sand can be counted? How big a space would a vigintillion of atoms fill? If the brain has three billion synapses, how many different thoughts can it have?

He was also the most obviously neurotic person I'd ever met, compelled yet afraid to bring up his questions in class: a brilliant actor with stage-fright, the fear betrayed by the slight hitch in every movement while he clowned and charmed his way through class. The uncertainty stayed with him even as he pursued me down the hall after class with one more brain teaser, yet another mathematical joke: Have you heard the one about the prisoners who told after dinner jokes by number only? That night's comedian would call out "Number Two Hundred Forty Five," and everyone would laugh. The new prisoner tried it one night to groans from the audience. He asked his cellmate later if number five hundred twelve wasn't a good joke. Yeah, the cellmate answered, but you didn't tell it right.

Donovan would add the sound effects as if he were a stand-up comic, a barumpty-bump for the drum roll after the punch line, an open-mouthed hiss in the back of his throat sounding uncannily like applause and cheers from a large and distant amphitheater audience.

At first I resisted, but Donovan was persistent. I yielded and started laughing. I didn't stop for years. Given the even-handedness of my life since my mother's death, I felt I'd been let back into the Magic Kingdom. We finally gave up the teacher-student charade. Passion makes straw of pedagogical distance.

I never completely gave up achieving, though Donovan tried to interfere with the habit. He both loved my ambition and competed with it. And our impulsive, mad marriage— one phosphorescent month after we met—might have distracted a less maniacally determined person. I stayed up later, got up earlier, disentangled myself from his black-haired arms, left him in the cave of our bedroom, and went to solve problems. I got the job at Stony Brook and, with my father's help, we bought a house on the beach. I sprinted around the tenure track.

For the first year, Donovan met me every day for lunch on campus. Even though I was often tired—weighed down with coffee sludge, committees, exams to grade—and he had given up on going to school, was sliding into inherited despair, neither of us could keep our hands occupied with the brown paper bags and plastic wrap. Even in public, on a park bench at noon, we reached out for each other's bodies as if they were parts of our own which we had misplaced years ago, had been desiring for more than just this lifetime.

Donovan was staying home all the time, writing poetry, walking on the beach, even in winter, when sand was driven into his skin and filled his beard like salt-preserved snow. I schooled myself in how to substitute pencil for flesh again.

By the fourth year of our marriage, when Donovan began having phantom pains and nightmares, I was already psychically divorced, although I left my body in the marriage for safekeeping. The symmetry of the relationship was gone; the dynamics had become unstable. Although I knew with my mind Donovan had his own locus of grief, I didn't understand that it, in conjunction with my own, would form a parabola no one could graph.

You may ask why I didn't put up more resistance, either to the marriage or to its end? I can best explain by saying that the whole thing—meeting, love, marriage, dissolution— seemed as inevitable to me as the merging of parallel lines at infinity.

Sometimes in late afternoon I take Galen into town to the grocery store or bank. It always seems it has taken all day to get around to going out. We are reluctant to go even then. The grocery store forces confrontations, but I have found a checker who isn't interested in anything but the price of beans, which he knows without looking it up in the cellophane booklet. After we come home we put things away, I call for George or maybe we take a walk to find him. The nights come on fast now. Usually we just fix dinner and settle in to read until bedtime. Modern instruments no longer hold our interest.

I am walking up to the cabin on a warm fall day with the blessing of the sun and the acridity of fallen leaves filling my senses. I have on jeans and my red flannel shirt. My face has a slight autumnal sunburn in this dream.

I reach for the doorknob but see that the door is already open.

It's the way so many nightmares and horror movies begin, you wonder later why you didn't just turn around and walk away. But you know you couldn't at the time, anymore than you could resist the compulsion of birth. So I push the door open.

It's my cabin all right, just a little different: more modern; more windows and light. Suddenly it's night and the comfort of sun-sharpened leaves is gone. I look toward the room where all along the light has been on and the water running. It's the bathroom moved dream-logically from the center of the house to just inside the front door.

Now is when the something terrible is going to happen.

A woman leans over the sink. She's washing her face. I walk toward the bathroom to be sure that really is my blue bathrobe she's wearing so comfortably. I need to see her haunches better; I need to see my slippers on her feet.

She hears me and straightens up. She comes out of the bathroom drying her face. She's coming out to welcome me to my own house. When she finishes patting her face dry I can see there is no mistake.

She is me.

Her face is round, white like the full moon, and completely bloodless, like the rest of her. She is remote, celestial, an unreachable and sickeningly familiar terrain.

She gestures slightly, fatally, with the towel, and I step into her living room, drawn into the most frigidly passionate embrace in the whole world.

I wake up, it's still dark, I'm paralyzed.

Every morning is like this until Thanksgiving morning when, through the dark before the dawn of the holiday, I can see Donovan's car in my driveway. He sings a Van Morrison song in my kitchen. I lie on my back a little while, letting the tears slide into my ears. I can't prove this, but I have faith that not one Pilgrim had as strong a sense of deliverance as I have now.

I stand in the kitchen door in my blue bathrobe, knowing Donovan knows as well as I do—and I don't use that phrase casually—that I am there. He is still singing, though—"You my brown-eyed girl"—and arranging things on the enamel tin top of the kitchen table. He dances a little with his body, keeping the beat but with a curious hesitation, a kind of jink of left leg and shoulder on the downbeat, a physical stutter that is his alone and, to me, deeply sweet and funny. He has coffee, cream, croissants, a ham, stuffing ingredients, butter, mushrooms, and real strawberries piled up outside their bag. Coffee grounds and cream are already spilled and puddled together on the table.

He has on jeans, broken-down tennis shoes, and a nylon jacket slick with unwashing. The seat of his jeans hangs a little too low for his rear-end, which I can see now as with X-ray vision is, despite the excess stomach, high and hard, just a little rounded. My hands curl themselves in its shape. He is running to fat, a sloven in every way. Yet he carries with him grace. Donovan is the one person in my world I could never have made up.

Still singing, he lifts the open cream carton up high and in a diving gesture pours a dollop in a white ceramic mug of hot French roast coffee. He swoops around to me, changing his song to "You my blue-eyed girl" as he hands me the mug.

Donovan makes inarticulate comforting sounds and holds me, rocking me just a little, not enough to spill the coffee I'm holding behind his back.

"Amelia, my glittering, icy wife," he says to me, "everything will be all right. I am here to save you from yourself."

"Donovan," I say gulping and sniffling like a kindergartner, "that's not a joke."

"There, there, my honey," he says. "Where would you ever have been without me?"

"You arrogant pig," I say while blowing my nose. To a Virginian, it is an extravagant freedom to be able to call someone whatever you want.

"Did I make you and mar you, like liquor did Macbeth's porter?" Donovan asks.

By grace, we are back where we started. For once, I accept his presence for the gift it is; I am willing to relinquish explanations, reassurances, all the abstract and symbolic persiflage means nothing. He had not been here, now he is.

"It's six in the morning, Donovan." I start to cry again. "And here you are, in my kitchen in the Adirondacks."

"It's six in the morning," he repeats like a lyric, "on Thanksgiving and I am here."

He holds me against his chest, enfolded in mercy. We slide down so that we are crouched together in the doorway. George lies in the bedroom behind me and Galen is beside Donovan, on the kitchen floor, her welcome already given while I dreamed.

"I thought I'd never see you again." I collapse still farther against him.

The dogs simultaneously drop their heads to the floor with a whump. They no longer resist the comfort.

This is terrifyingly easy," I say to Donovan in bed. We are making love for the first time in six months and, although the conscious memory is long gone, it is as if we were singing a favorite song which we'd forgotten but which suddenly came back, every word, every inflection of it.

"High wire artists never forget," he says. He has his own comparisons.

He has no clothes on. I have on underpants and the little sleeveless t-shirt I sleep in. He pinches my nipples through the shirt. The pinch is a little too rough, the tug a little too hard. We admire the way my nipples stand out against the t- shirt.

"Pretty," he says. He touches my forehead and then my breast. "Brains and beauty."

"Donovan McLarty, Explorer," I say. "Founder of the fire, banked, on the marble floor inside the ivory tower."

Donovan gets up and rummages through the top dresser drawer. He comes back with my long string of natural pearls. I loop them once tight around my neck and let the rest hang down. We laugh at how funny they look against a thermal t-shirt.

"Glamorous," I say.

Donovan dives for me and bites my neck hard. The whisky smell on his breath is rich, years of Scotch overriding all other possibilities. His sweat is diesel. I push up against him and he turns me over. I lift my hips up and he pushes my underpants to one side and comes inside me, biting the skin at the base of my skull, covering my back.

When I wake up the first time, I am curled on my right side and Donovan is curled behind me. His arm is thrust up between my breasts and my arms are crossed over it, holding him in a corpse's embrace. The pearls are between my teeth.

Donovan is singing in the kitchen again. I can hear it just a little above the sound of heavy fall rain thundering on the tin roof. I go out to Donovan just as I am. I push him against the table and straddle his jeaned crotch.

"I may have to fuck you again," I say.

"Your cunt is first class," Donovan says. He holds me against him and grinds. Suddenly he shoves me backwards. "I'm going to make you scream," he says. He pushes me into the living room.

I pull him onto the rug. I have one foot on the couch, one on the old chest in front of it. Our fucking is as rough and rolling and inevitable as the sea at night. I call Donovan's name high, like a sea bird.

Thanksgiving dinner starts with strawberries, caviar and French bread. We eat these and drink two bottles of champagne in bed while the turkey roasts. We wake up just in time for golden, spitting turkey. The turkey spread requires our getting out of bed and seems a little Puritanical compared to the appetizers. But we are as hungry as football players at summer camp and we eat heartily, our bodies reeking of each other, our crotches warm and soft and used. We eat mostly in each other's laps. It is such a sexy occasion, we wonder why anyone ever invites family. We take the last bottle of wine into the living room and lie on the sofa tangled in satisfaction.

We have one sour moment.

"Forgive me yet?" Donovan says. He has reached inside my half-buttoned flannel shirt and is holding my breast.

I pull back. I have forgotten without forgiving and I am surprised to be reminded, as well as being surprised I'm surprised.

"I just wish this, Amelia," he says, "I wish I knew which of the transgressions was the real one."

"Booze. Women. The inability to find anything satisfactory for long. The way your eyes hooded over as a falcon's will as you began to hate me more and more. The way they are hooding over now," I say.

I am helpless, as I always was—his eyes go stony; the snows continue to blow in my soul. He drops his head forward and looks at me sideways, a bird of prey who hasn't quite decided yet whether it is prey or mate he has in his sights.

"You know what I see in your eyes?" he says. "Icy air, billowing, so clear it is blue, Arctic. So clear I may fall and fall through it and you will never know I am there. I hate it more than anything about you. My beloved Amelia—smart, wisecracking, loving: my buoy—goes North, back to her Ice Kingdom, dragging me along, the boy with the ice chip lodged in his heart."

"I believe ice melts," I say. "I may be capable of going numb, but I have never believed being a queen of ice meant I rule over anything worthwhile."

At this point we both remember that this conversation started out being about Donovan's sins. He puts into practice a useful trick: he can forgive himself. Like George, he virtually forgives himself before he has done the deed for which he might otherwise have felt guilt.

"Another lifetime," he says. He waves the whole past away and puts his hand back on my breast. His face is animated, a boy who remembers he already has the toy he most covets. Life and joy have returned. "Kiss, kiss," he says. He smacks his lips together lightly.

"Oh, my soul," I say, a Southernism that can be taken literally in this case. I tangle my cold fingers in his chest hair.

The next night we are at the grocery store. Donovan doesn't want turkey again; he wants steak. We have had a small argument about who is going to pay. It is a familiar argument and my reaction is familiar. I believe he is right— he has paid enough for food, but suppose I want fish or duck? Is it necessary I pay for what he wants?

This is an undecidable problem. At least there is no solution that doesn't strike me as trivial. Donovan has accused me of Protestantism and stalked off down an aisle, carrying the basket. I'm doing a study of the varieties of pasta when he comes back. I don't wonder for more than one variety where it is he got the money to buy the feast in the first place. Cab; borrowed; woman? He takes my hand. I could weep where I stand when I see him coming toward me: his big, manly body and the little basket of food in his hand; the way he has come back to me.

"Who is this I see," he says, "this tall, blonde woman, clearly intelligent, nearly pretty, standing tragicomically in spaghetti? I love your dark and coagulated soul, Amelia. Even that. I wouldn't recognize you at all if you didn't bring me down every single time I'm on a high flight."

On the way home, steak on the back seat of the Saab, Donovan talks about what we will do as soon as we sell the Stony Brook house.

"A farm up here might be a little rough, though we'll do it if you want," he offers. "I'll do the garden. I can see you casting grain to the chickens."

"And the dogs," I say, "will naturally run from one to the other."

I am driving. Donovan has his hand inside my coat and shirt, holding my breast again. I feel his cock through his pants when I'm not making turns or shifting gears.

"And you: a bay mare," he says.

"That I ride to town to do errands."

"I ride a . . ."

"Tractor."

"Wife of my soul."

The tears are melting down my face now, neither impeded nor propelled by anything I do. I pull into the drive. The dogs bound up, each on a side though mixed up. Galen is on my side, George on Donovan's. Donovan pulls me across the hand brake and into his coat's embrace.

"What is it, my sweet?"

"The farm is so nice," I say by way of nonsensical explanation. "I've always believed there is such a thing as a nice life."

"You had a chilly childhood, love," he says. "That doesn't mean your permanent residence is the tundra."

"I know that in my mind, Donovan," I say. "But what about frost damage?"

Donovan jiggles me, the way one does a baby.

"Any horticulturist will tell you," he says, "if the plant has only died back to the ground, under the right conditions it will—sometimes slowly—regenerate."

"There is something seriously wrong with the farm, Donovan. To some, it might represent a dream that is, in fact, possible if they work hard for it. To me it lacks something essential. It doesn't even qualify as a fairy tale in the way people generally mean it, because it lacks redemption, the reality factor—horror—of a real fairy tale—the fear, the threat, the likelihood of failure."

But Donovan is already out of the car and doesn't hear me. I pull myself together and get out of the car. Galen is disappointed, I can tell: she got me and not her Magic Man. But she covers. Well-bred, as if she too had been raised in Virginia, she wags her tail apparently as delighted as if I'd been whom she wanted. George isn't such a dissembler, but he finds substitution easy, a trick one learns obligatorily, to get by. He trots toward the house robustly, merrily, behind Donovan who shuffles and jinks toward the house, embodying everything I understand of humor and grace.

I follow along behind George, both of us dogging Donovan into the cabin. Donovan leaves the groceries on the table and fixes a drink. I remember—or my stomach does—it will now be hours before we actually eat. With Donovan it is always like this—the great promise of food that will, in fact, be delicious, but will also, equally as factually, be cooked and served on his schedule. And one can never quite tell how far down the freight train that moment will come.

I put the groceries away and go into the living room where Donovan is lying on the sofa, drinking his Scotch and reading the Collected Yeats he brought with him.

"Is there a caboose of now?" I ask him.

"Huh?"

I feed logs into the woodstove and sweep up the bark. I throw that in too and it submits in one fast blossom of flame.

"Do you think we have a prayer? When we both feel marriage is like being held by terrorists?"

He puts a finger in his place in Yeats and watches me.

He comes over to the woodstove and crouches beside me at the open door, takes both my hands.

"But, Amelia, what is the alternative? Not to be disturbed like that—to keep your life pristine—is like staying in the womb."

"But at least you're alone there; you have privacy—and sovereignty."

Donovan laughs. "In the womb? Are you kidding? Your mother had control of that."

I have decided I'll cook dinner and let him have his Yeats a while longer. I get out the soup pot and start a steak and vegetable stew, set the table with the big, flat soup bowls, go outside for wood.

The dogs are outside and thrilled in their separate ways to see me. There is a just-past full moon pouring through the pines. I'm rising, I can tell, lifted up by the intoxication of being understood. I look at the dogs and at my skis, leaning against the house. Galen, seated, wags the farthest joint of her tail across the snow. I already have my ski shoes on. I snap the skis onto the toes and we all three head into the woods, past the cemetery of the garden.

The snow isn't very deep and I hit bare patches, so I ski toward the road. It's still not icy there because my car is the only one that comes down the road anymore, but it is packed enough to prevent its disintegrating even over the rocks in the road. I ski fast, airily, as if flying through the white light all around me: the moon, the snow.

When I get to the paved road, the snow becomes treacherous— either iced over or nonexistent. I whistle the dogs back from where they are already heading down the main road. George may be following an urge to go out on the town. He goes at his happy-go-lucky pace, stops to check on me occasionally. Galen, though, is going on a long and mysterious quest, her elegant nose forever pointed forward. She is very nearly lost in the moonlight and shadow. Though hang-tailed disappointed, they come back to me when I call.

From outside I can see the lights are all on in the living room. I adjust to their artificiality by going into the house through the bedroom, carrying wood. I have an urge to take Donovan outside and make love like animals in the snow which I think I'll satisfy indoors but just as savagely. My mouth can still feel the shape of his cock inside it from this afternoon before the grocery store and I can still taste the oceanic flavor of his semen at the top of my throat.

I go through the kitchen with a sense of urgency. This must be like what animals feel when they want to breed. I don't think I can stand not having him inside me for the length of time it will take to get out of my clothes. As pressing a need as it is, I also want to stop in the kitchen and throw together a baked Alaska; I want to speed by my desk and quickly finish off that problem that will guarantee me tenure; I want to sing an aria from a tragic opera. And I'm pretty sure I can.

"Donovan," I shout, quite loud enough to stir a corpse, certainly loud enough to knock a little more mortar out from between the logs of the walls.

But not enough to disturb Donovan, who, with every light in the living room on full, is dead drunk on the sofa. I can tell by the way his body is tossed on the sofa, victim of a hit-and-run. No amount of calling will make a difference. No need of mine will effect a rescue.

"Donovan," I say, a reminder to me of how many times this has happened in my married life. I stack the wood next to the stove.

He moves uncomfortably on the sofa. I stand over him.

"Emmy," he says in a strangely officious voice, about to make a pronouncement, to announce a Papal bull maybe. "Emmy, don't climb the steps into your white mind."

I have been sitting at my desk for an unknown amount of time. Donovan is still asleep, a casualty at least for the night. I have been watching him sleep and reenacting what must have happened when I was gone.

He read Yeats, getting from the poetry what consolation Donovan can ever have. He read some aloud, stood and declaimed "Under Ben Bulben." He rose higher and higher on the tide of aesthetic passion. He went out to the kitchen to let it spill over onto me, to magnify his pleasure. He had his arms out, book set aside, superfluous. He was ready to hold me in his bear arms while he boomed out another favorite: "Many ingenious lovely things are gone/That seemed sheer miracle to the multitude." He would stroke my thigh while he said it and it would seem Yeats meant us, the ingenious things who had once been "Protected from the circle of the moon/That tosses common things about."

"Ahh," he would have said, resonant, a rumble of pleasure, not the light satisfaction of a mere aesthete but of one who feels the poem all through his body. "Ah, Amelia." The smile would have taken over his face; the delight would have translated quite naturally from his body to mine.

Hideously, I was not there.

The light was on; soup bowls were on the table. Presence sufficiently implied to define a clear-cut case of absence.

Donovan, my warm, generous, mad husband. Who cannot stand abandonment, even the hint of it.

I have worked on this problem long enough to have succeeded in finding a solution: I have had pity. I know from the last seven months, I could do this again. If this is what he needs, I could have pity on him over and over. I think, for a period, this is the answer. It is cold comfort next to the desire I felt when I first came in, but we are all broken.

The phone rings and I go to the kitchen to answer. I cover Donovan with the army blanket on my way by.

A long distance woman's voice asks for Donovan. Virginia manners kick in.

"He can't come to phone right now. May I take a message?" I say.

"To whom am I speaking?" she asks.

She's got me on two scores now: I should have been the one to ask this question. And, much as I wish she sounded like a cheap young floozy, she is at least as old as I and as grammatical.

"To whom am I speaking?" I say. I know from watching girl fights in the public high school I'll never recover the advantage.

"Tell him I got home this afternoon and I'll wait up to hear from him tonight."

"Where can he call you?" I say, with something of the same feeling as when I walked in the door of the nightmare. She gives me my own phone number in Stony Brook. I write it on a card. "I'll tell him," I say.

I walk the length of the kitchen once, away from the living room door. Then I walk back. On my way to the living room I pick up a wine glass from the shelf.

I throw the glass against the woodstove. It breaks very satisfyingly. Good crystal will.

I'm so pleased with the sound I go back to the kitchen. This one I hurl like a javelin against the wall behind the sofa. Pow. It detonates as if it too craves shattering.

"Donovan," I say. He has started to move. He is puzzled by the glass shards on his blanket. He looks at me. "Your supper's ready."

I breeze back through the kitchen, stopping a moment to dump both ice cube trays into the soup bowls and then whooshing out of the house through the bedroom. Like the wine glass, I am propelled.

Outside I snap on the skis and fly. I can see Donovan at the house in my mind: the shadow of my husband stumbling into the ghostly kitchen as it appears against the screen of black tree trunks along my unguided trajectory.

"What the fuck?" he says. "Amelia?"

He sees the card propped behind his soup bowl. He picks it up and reads: "Call your whore." Beneath it is our phone number.

He sits down, deflated. He will wonder how he got himself into this mess, why he gave her my phone number, try to remember when he told her to expect him back, and wonder why he never told her he is married.

"I must be crazy," he says.

He resolves to do something or another—he'll have to think what—to make it up to one or both of us. This is a good one, this time.

Then he looks into the soup bowl and sees the ice cubes.

When I get back to the house it's completely dark. Donovan's car is gone. The winds of the night blow through my body. I think maybe he has just gone into town to a bar. We have fought before, have walked away before. Even when I knew for sure he'd be back, the desertion was always like stepping onto the wasteland, a long journey ahead, maybe a futile one or one that will fail, will end in death. His return always a reprieve, a rescue, a pardon from the sentence of crossing the steppe alone with inadequate provisions, the necessity of solving a problem that is intrinsically, invisibly flawed.

In the kitchen, next to the bowl of water, Donovan has left the card. On the other side of it he has written:

"Solitude is your whore. I never could compete. Eat his cold supper, drink his ice wine."

Too much Yeats, I think just before I lie down on the bed and am swallowed by sleep, still dressed and shivering.

CHAPTER FOUR:

Advent

Donovan never chops. His main function is burning, and he does that splendidly. After two days of firewood consumption, there is an awful lot of wood to be split today. That will have to wait for dawn.

Meantime, there are fall garden catalogs to catch up on, a pile of them, cool and sticking a little to the bare skin just above my knees. Could I, like an impractical Eskimo woman, cut a hole in the cold ground and drop in a hyacinth bulb on a string, fishing for spring? Through the bedroom door, in the dark of the living room, illuminated inwardly by its own purity, its freshness, is the mathematics problem. But even if I tried multiplying the kernel of f times the image of f, it wouldn't get me out of this fix.

I watch the driveway where Donovan's car used to be. I'm sitting on the edge of the bed with no clothes on, garden catalogs hand-hooked onto my down-sloping knees like schoolbooks. My ankles are crossed. After being asleep no more than an hour, I have woken up, gotten the catalogs from the kitchen and taken everything off. I don't know where the dogs are.

On top of the catalogs Donovan's note is pinned with both my thumbs: a mailing label, a banner. I have been here several hours but that still doesn't mean dawn. Already the winter hours need to be endured, planned; they have already turned metallic, industrial; technical and unwieldy, as they always do when Donovan is gone.

I'd be a fool not to admit he is essentially right about the solitude. One thing about my husband: he knows me. I would make this slight correction: solitude is less my lover than your legacy to me, Ma. Even though you were never comfortable with it yourself, you must still have had the sense to see a lust for loneliness might come in handy for your daughter, so you died a death so absolute and mysterious it created a vacuum around me, one Mother Nature could hate all she wanted, but She could never fill.

I'd like to attribute this sort of foresight to you anyway, Ma, because, otherwise, I'm pretty close to terminally confused about why you exited so radically, so dramatically in such silence and haste. I cannot believe I existed so little to you.

And I like to think you would catch me in the lie, too, the one about the vacuum. It's a wish really—a wish for a sort of simplicity, a fantasy the space around me is like that inside the domed glass jars containing a gold clock which never needs dusting or winding but simply ticks away its hours. I, on the contrary, am clogged with dust and the only person I've known in my adult life with any sort of key is Donovan.

I let the catalogs do as they have wished for so long and fall off my knees, but I still hold Donovan's note pinched between thumbs and forefingers, staring at it as if at an invitation I can't quite believe I've received.

Even if the state I live in isn't quite as pure as I might wish, there is still the legacy, real enough to keep my husband at bay. How am I supposed to address myself to this gift, after all these years? You left no instructions, Ma. When you deeded it to me I was much too young to give it back. And I'd always been taught to be polite about gifts:

don't drop them on the floor, say I already have one or wanted something else, hate the color. I knew not to make a face of any kind other than the one of pleased surprise caked on a bride's face at a shower and on the face of all well-bred children when handed anything in tissue. I knew not to behave in any way that would cause notice to be taken of you. I knew not to act up.

So, true to my training, I watch the driveway for an immeasurable amount of time. The wooden door is open and I am watching through the crystal-clean glass of the storm door—watching where Donovan's car was and where it had gone. I hold his note the whole time.

My legacy is with me here, too, like a particularly unattractive brooch affixed to my bare skin, or an ugly hair ornament twisted painfully into my hair forever. But I will wear it proudly, as if it were gold and garnets. Just what is the alternative?

Though Donovan had been gone some time before I came back from skiing and several hours have passed since then, I watch the red taillights of his car disappear across the snow and into the black again and again.

I lose track of the few days after Donovan leaves. Time, no longer daily as it had been before his advent and abandonment, alternates between being manufactured and then turning suddenly magnificent: blurred and mystical. One day, lifting the sledgehammer is impossible; the next there are, miraculously, perfectly split logs and neatly piled kindling.

Then there is a little more clarity to the day I wake up inspired as if I've been vouchsafed a vision. I go on a fall cleaning spree as on a mission. I do floors, walls, light fixtures. I do windows inside and out. I wash all my clothes and all the household laundry, including dog blankets. I find a sock of Donovan's that hasn't been exposed to the washing machine for some time. I wash that. I find some notes of his that look like attempted poems, a couple of pens the ends of which have been chewed, his toothbrush. I'm at a loss as to what to do with them, so I put them in a grocery bag which I put in the dining room, now too cold to use.

After everything is clean, I go through another spell I don't remember very well. I remember a blistering anger. I remember days of skiing for hours cursing his name, panting the curses through the silver birches.

At the end I understand Donovan could no more help abandoning me than you could, Ma. I can no more stop this pain than I could have not thrown the wine glasses.

But if you couldn't help it and he couldn't and I couldn't, what is left for me to do? Is there any point in trying to learn to live with a television that shows only snow? I am pretty sure I could learn to live with it, but the question is, you know, is there any point?

I naturally unplug the television and move it into the dining room.

I see more clearly what the larger mission might be. Knowing that a house exists largely as extension of its chatelaine's body, I start to imagine I can houseclean the soul, factor out the junk and go on: clean, linear.

Without confusion or profusion, without hesitation or indecision.

Every day's schedule can then be followed without compromise or negotiation. Everything will be done.

The dogs will be fed at the same time every day; no more stray nuggets.

Transactions and Proceedings of the American Math Society will get all ten articles.

No more apologies. Everything checked off the list. Body and mind clean, working synchronously.

Isometric exercises to keep this thinning body taut.

An orderly, quiet, calm life—recognizable, pale blue. The way a mathematician ought to live.

No more moments of hideous frustration when one simply writes off the day and goes for drinks with one's husband. No more hideous passion.

An endless sense of accomplishment: continuous, not discrete. A settling in, an acceptance of the barren.

A giving up of the good fight with relief and a tiny, distinguished, affordable regret, like salt and pepper hair. Cleanliness and order.

But everyone who aims for infinity must start at one; everyone has to pay the dues. And don't forget: for some of us there are debts to pay first, some negative numbers to pass through before we even reach zero. I have lost the ability to eat and sleep.

They were subtracted as soon as Donovan's whore called. As soon as I heard a woman's voice saying his name, my intestine doubled up and knotted. It is not exactly nausea, more like what people actually mean when they say the bottom of their stomach fell. It doesn't fall; it hardens sickeningly. This isn't my first experience with this. When women started calling for him at our house (is it "theirs" now? This is, incredibly, not entirely a facetious question), it did feel like nausea. Once I vomited. It was a letter I found, carefully and sentimentally preserved in his novel notebook where I was unforgivably poking for evidence of his day. Luckily, he wasn't home and no one knew how sick it made me. His drinking had worsened—or improved, I suppose, to him—so much that I don't think he knew I knew anything. I knew enough to know it was no good to rage at him.

The one nice thing about the sickness now, after Thanksgiving, is this is the last time I'll have to go through it. I just have to go through it this one time and then I'll be free.

The problem is I'm not completely sure how I'm going to accomplish this. Before, the only thing that could cure me was Donovan's presence, the comfort of the dark warm cave of his body and his generous, meaningless reassurance. Now that I am minus even that ambiguous solution, what is there? Time? The only analog I can remember is the helpless feeling I had at your funeral, where I also threw up, though Father says he doesn't remember.

So, one way or another, the sickness will be over soon and that is nice. It is also nice that the nausea has a different nature; it is familiar enough now that my relationship to it is clinical, an almost abstract recognition of the knot tied in fairly complex configurations in my intestine. After I have gotten rid of whatever it was I last tried to eat, there is relief for a little while, until I try to eat again, or until I think of him with her again, which I do every morning.

I wake up every morning at four, imagining her in his arms. I have imagined these scenes many times before — every time he left. But this time I have her voice as well as his in my mind. He would be fucking her sleepily then, from behind; he would be saying her name and not mine as he comes; she would answer; and then he would pull her close, her back against his chest, and go back to sleep. I lie on my bed every morning as if tied to the bedposts and imagine this scene. My guts knot. I submit to the discipline.

As with the ugly jewels I wear forever in my imagination, what is the choice, exactly? I want him; I love him. His intellect, his talent, his humor make a kind of magic to which I feel humbly apprenticed. If he sends himself up in smoke now, am I anywhere near ready to take over the job?

He is dead to me, but somewhere, to someone else, he is explodingly alive, then covering her in the blanket of his body.

I accept as my covering the blanket of snow falling daily on my house. Two weeks after Thanksgiving a snow in the night blocks the storm door closed. I have opened the wooden door and am watching the snow in the dark. It is four-thirty in the morning and I am waiting for the sickness to finish running over me and leave me in peace on the bed for the buzzards of divorce. I do understand by this time the sickness isn't fatal; it won't kill me, at least not anytime soon. I'm waiting for the vision of Donovan to fade in the blackness again.

When it does — or dims at least — I get up, put on my blue robe and slippers, go to the bathroom, start a bath. While the bath runs, I go around the house turning on the lights, beating back the dark with extraordinary futility, starting in the kitchen. I let the dogs out on the way. I think I have all the lights on when I remember the dining room, cold and closed. I go back through the kitchen and turn on the dining room lights. I am suddenly struck with admiration for the grocery bag of Donovan—the one I put his sock in.

It strikes me as a revelation—not just one brown bag, but a program, a mission.

I go back to the bathroom, turn off the water, and begin packing things into my vanity case. I put in the facial masque and nail polish remover, cosmetic luxuries. I clamp the case closed and put it on the dining room table.

This starts to satisfy me, but there is clearly more to be done with this project. I roll up my bathrobe sleeves, find an empty box, and begin in the kitchen packing up the things one would chose first when moving or having a yard sale. I pack the Bundt pan and electric juicer. I'm delighted to be able to pack the food processor in its original box. It goes in a dining room corner. I pack three boxes of books and all my summer clothes. For a little while, this will have to be enough.

I let some water out of the tub, turn the hot water back on, put a cinnamon roll in the toaster oven. I read the Post-It on the refrigerator reminding me to drink water and I obey it. I know what is wrong with me, although only an emotional flu, can lead to dehydration as fast as any case of amoebic dysentery can.

Somewhere along the line, as my marriage rotted, I came up with a ritual of grieving. It includes baths, eating sweet, soft foods, reading women's magazines, and the right amount of alcohol. I pour a cup of coffee and top it with Scotch. After a little consideration, I turn off all the lights in the house again, even though it is everlastingly dark outside. I light a candle in the bathroom, close the door, and turn off that light too.

I lay my body, shaking from the strain of not eating or sleeping, into the white womb.

One thing I've discovered about the body is that it has an unfortunate capacity to remember. Almost as soon as he left, my mind couldn't recall what Donovan looks like, but my skin has memorized his skin. My hair still has his hand in it. My sleeping body shapes itself around the memory of him in bed, leaves his side free. Somewhere in the dark of my mind it is as if on some other planet Donovan is forever pushing inside me.

Here, in the cold porcelain world, I contend with the idea that two weeks before Christmas, more than two weeks after we made love for the last time, Donovan's come is still inside me, having transcended the membranes of my cunt and worked its way into my blood where it pumps from heart to head to feet to lungs in a takeover that has me wondering if this is even the same corporation.

The panic begins, the doom of never being able to reach Donovan, or anyone else who might help.

One plus one is two. Two take away one leaves one, but not the same one as before—a different one, changed.

The next day is Monday, and I wait, patiently in my opinion, for regular business hours. I call Galen to come with me and she does, sitting upright in the back seat, erect as if balancing her visiting hat, ready to go calling. The first stop is the realtor's office.

"May I speak to Mrs. Greene?" I ask the receptionist. The office is festooned with Christmas.

"Mrs. Greene isn't here," the receptionist says. She has a sprig of plastic holly in her hair.

"Gone to lunch already?" I say. I thought I had waited the exact amount of time to catch the grandmotherly realtor conscientiously coming to work.

"Oh, she won't be back till March or April," the woman says.

"Spring?" I say.

The woman looks a little concerned. I realize that I sound untowardly incredulous. I do find Mrs. Greene's absence incredible, as a matter of fact. I hadn't understood how much I had counted on her to remonstrate, to cluck over what I am about to do. She had never liked the situation, but she had implied a promise to keep an eye on me.

Is this what we would call keeping an eye?

"Flown South, has she?" I say, a bit of the hard-boiled detective about me.

Of course, she hadn't said she was going to watch over me the rest of my life.

"Can someone else help you?"

"Anyone," I say.

A man who might also be the accountant for the office pulls my lease out of the file.

"Through May, ma'am?" he says.

"Mathematicians often can't add," I say. I'm jovial now, friendly. "What is the total?"

"You may mail in the payment monthly, of course," he says.

"But I don't want to," I say. "I want to pay now. Would you like for me to work the calculator for you?"

Ma'am, he can see, has suddenly turned testy. He adds up five month's rent and gives me the total. I write the check.

"Would you please attach a note to the lease that the house is occupied through May and no one needs to look after it? If I need anything, I'll call," I say.

He makes a note of this.

"Yes, ma'am," he says.

Young male accountants have no curiosity. I think about kicking him for not asking me what I'm up to, but he thinks—and he might well be right—I would have slugged him if he had.

"Another great leap of ignorance," a voice in my head says. I'm in the car and I look at Galen. It isn't my own voice

I hear. It is yours. I'm shocked by it, but almost immediately I feel accompanied. You, gently gray-haired as you never were in life, shake your head in my mind. The stupidity of young men, the shocking lack of perspicacity. We, you and I, are justifiably judgmental and we laugh.

Next I stop at the electric company. A rocky face, female, acts nonchalant, as if every day someone offers large amounts of money to keep the lights burning for an indefinite period of time. Nevertheless, the amount she suggests as a deposit seems exorbitant to me. I pay it, order a tank of oil for the furnace, get groceries, stop at the post office, and go home.

Snow is now a secure part of the landscape. It seems inevitable, built-in. I drive at just the right speed to achieve forward progress without going so fast as to cause a big problem if I have to stop. When I try to imagine what summer felt like on my skin, what the air smelled like, or the softly, gorgeously dying colors of early fall, or the taste of turkey and the fullness of champagne inside me, I get a sense of vertigo, a hopelessness over the body's ability to really bring anything back. Even garden catalogs are futile. Snow it is. I fishtail around the curve just before my cabin.

Inside, I check my face in the corroded bathroom mirror. I am looking to see what the electric company saw there. I can't see that I look crazed. I only look mute as the Hunter's moon.

In some sense, of course, I have always been on the widow's walk of the soul, always getting ready for Donovan to leave, thinking, "Well, this is a project I'll do when he's gone"—learning to sew, or cleaning behind the refrigerator.

After I have put everything away, I sit at my desk. My intent is to work on the problem that will guarantee me tenure, but I push it to the other end of the library table as if it physically repulsed me. I take two sheets of stationery out of the drawer and line up the corners. I wonder whose name I'll put on it. There is some tired white sun on my back coming through the window behind me, but the dark room I face into is cool, in gloom. I wait.

"Dear Mom," I write. "I've just come back from renting the cabin for the winter and paying a sizable deposit on the utilities. I filled out a form at the post office to hold all mail that doesn't fit in the box. Unfortunately, I forgot the phone company. Everything else is checked off my list. Do you think it is significant that the phone is the one thing I forgot?"

I stop writing. I'm struggling to find the right tone for the letter. I am chagrined: I've forgotten how to write to you. Do you expect efficiency? Or do I get sympathy from you? Are you psychologically savvy? Writing is a different order of magnitude from mind talking. But your talking to me has opened this door.

It has been a long time since I wrote, certainly since before my marriage, probably before graduate school. Have I written since high school? Maybe not. Maybe I decided I was finished with you then, that it would be embarrassing to write to one's dead mother from college, as if one carried a particularly morbid teddy bear.

But as a child it had been easy and quite possibly necessary for me to write. When you died I was six and had spent most of my life up till then living with you in the castle of your imagination. A child-like woman yourself, you were often more my playmate than my mother. Every day you furnished the rooms of the castle with some new surprise. Whenever I asked you to, you would get out the iron to iron the remnant of my baby blanket so that it was warm when I held it against my face. Then you got sick; there was hysterical dancing with Father; and then the cold. You had died of breast cancer, dead six weeks after the diagnosis.

The letters were my idea. I could already read, write, count, add, and subtract. Father implied his encouragement when he came to say good night once and found me propped up in bed and writing furiously. When he saw that the pulpy, blue-lined sheets were addressed to "Mommy, Heaven," did he think I'd taken Virginia manners to a new level: of course, when a loved one is absent, one corresponds? He was already worn by then, I think, and most of what I got from him I read.

I was writing that night, as I usually did, an account of two or three things I'd done that day, probably in school. The letters weren't ever very expressive, I don't think. I don't think I'd ever been a very emotional child—more imperious. By the time of the letters, Father and I lived in Grandmother's house and everything had become as remote as the large, high-ceilinged distant rooms. The letters were like the light I could see at night through the transom window above the bedroom door—remote, coming from an unidentifiable source but still comforting, as is anything that has to be. The letters were a lifeline, however questionable.

It wasn't as if no one took care of me then. Grandmother's housekeeper gave me Cokes and snacks after school. Grandmother herself wasn't directly interested in me and taught her stern lessons by example: solitude, nature, power.

I rarely wrote to you about Grandmother. You two were so different you seemed a bad chemical mix—dangerous— or numbers from entirely different base systems whose interaction would be all wrong. It felt like my responsibility to keep you apart. It wasn't a light one, even under the circumstances of your being dead. I was a teenager when Grandmother died.

I wrote to you the whole time. When adolescence steamrollered me I sometimes wrote a twenty or thirty page epistle to you. I realized even then how fortunate I was: most girls my age hated their mothers, but you were fair, sympathetic, liberal—what with being a figment of my imagination and all. I imagined your beauty had increased with age, you acquired the precious, hard-won evanescence of the aging magnolia blossom, the earned gorgeousness of a spent parchment rose.

All along I imagined you near me; we were often standing next to each other in my mind. I was the adored little blonde girl inside the circle of your arms first (this one may even have been a picture) and then I was a gangly blue-jeaned teenager with long straight hair next to a dark-haired, skirted and cardiganed sixties version of you. Now you are light-haired, your face full of humor and character as well as the soft beauty, and you look at me, taller and thinner and blonde but still your daughter. Though I have made some peculiar decisions about what to do with my life, you regard them with a wry acceptance. As I conjure you, I add the last detail: your beauty had always been set off by the dark green gloss of humor.

"I don't believe I ever introduced you to Donovan," I write, "but you would have liked him. He was the husband."

You would have laughed over "the husband." The definite article would have tickled you.

"You would have kept Glenfiddich in the house for him."

You would have, if you'd ever had the chance.

For the next week I write to you, Ma, through most of the day and into the sleepless nights. The dogs keep vigil, watching or sleeping next to me as I write as furiously as I ever did as a child.

I write at my desk sometimes, propped up in bed others, and several times I put on my coat and hat and go out to sit in the wooden armchair on the deck, the pen sliding through my gloved grip. Once I try writing in the dining room, but the cold in there is even more bitter than outside. In the darkest part of the night or morning, the bathtub is the only place that provides enough protection for my project, writing pad on sloppy knees, illumination from candles in tall silver holders on the toilet tank.

The dogs travel with me as I go from one perch to another. They watch as I understand the project of my life has been to be alone. I have come into this solitude as if going home. I come to see the error of ever having thought of myself as a social being, however successful I had been at it. I might at some other time have even said I was afraid of being alone. But in filling you in on the missing years, I can see that friends I told you about in high school had vanished with no trace of regret on my part as soon as I left for college. I had trouble remembering their names and, even in the case of Christmas cards, couldn't imagine their lives now.

When I first begin this project I try to keep a semblance of order, of normalcy to my day. I try to cook meals at the right time and eat them, but I'll twirl a bite of angel hair pasta and then leave the fork on the plate and pick up the pen, having remembered a detail—an Easter vacation at a college girlfriend's house, seeing Tintagel on my graduation trip to England, a green jacquard Chinese dress I bought for a dance. The food is even less appetizing cold—indissoluble lumps of shredded Parmesan, pasta that, like eels, returns to its uncooked state if left out of the boiling water too long.

One time I leave the laundry out of the washer for the entire cycle when I remember the name of an obscure boyfriend in graduate school whose grandmother would not allow me to visit for Passover due to my being a shiksa. The dog food not infrequently ends up sodden in the water bowl when I fail to notice that my aim is off. George studies the situation from time to time, looking from the bag of Alpo to first the empty food bowl, then the overstuffed water bowl. He is mystified, still good-natured. Galen, made a little more nervous by it all, lifts her paws up high when she follows me from kitchen to living room; then she returns to the kitchen, clicks her nails against the linoleum as she circles the water bowl wondering if anything in this situation can be salvaged.

The woodpile is too dangerous for me to approach in this absent state and mathematics can be damned. Soon everything can be. I give myself over to the project. The snow has begun to fall almost without end. Its hushed sizzle is a kind of music that accompanies my work. At some point I am persuaded by it to put even the radio in the storeroom.

I tell you about the men I'd met in college. It's easy to meet them when one is a mathematics major: most of my classmates were exclusively male by the time I hit senior year. They were serious and unkempt and their names came at the end of the alphabet. They didn't quite know what to do with me outside the classroom. They were often sweetly shy men.

Some weren't; some asked me out. I went, but the evenings were frustrating to us both. I would want to either discuss a math problem or go to party and for some— the engineering-minded—a date, like mathematics, was functional, and sex alone was rarely a good enough goal, an elaborate enough structure. They wanted to find out whether or not I was marriage material. It became clear enough to everyone involved that I was not.

Until Donovan, my life looked in my mind as if staged: a crowd scene with people dressed in gray, moving along with some purpose—some jolly, some not—with me downstage, stage right; still, fawn-colored in a narrow spotlight, alone. Even yours and my relationship had been private, a club that admitted only us two, and, like any good country club, compelling in proportion to its exclusivity.

I didn't have anything against relationships. It wasn't as if I didn't understand that warmth existed, was desirable. It was as if some crucial factor for making an emotional connection was simply missing. But it turned out to be stored, not absent, and it flamed through its lead-lined box fast enough when I met Donovan.

"You would be the first to understand," I write, "that it only took one month of Donovan chasing me down the hall with one more question, one more problem, before we were going to movies we talked all the way through and danced home from, before we realized we could not study together because our hands would fly up from our books and papers to each other's bodies, before we found ourselves suddenly married. My heart was stupefied with pleasure. We were like puppies from the same litter who had lost each other but now were found.

"I took him to Virginia to meet Father, but they didn't get along. Donovan broke the cut-glass vase Grandmother used to put japonica in and Father told me as I was leaving that of all the men I'd dated, this was the one he would least have wanted me to marry. I didn't know he'd noticed the other men.

"We didn't go back there often, but Father did help us buy the house in Stony Brook when I got the job. Donovan kept on driving the cab for a couple of years. Then he decided to try writing a novel. I made enough money for us to live on. Neither of us doubted the prospective brilliance of his novel.

"Does that sound like a book coming up over the horizon or what?"

My hand is cramped and I am finally tired now that I have gotten to my marriage. It also happens to be sometime late in the night of who knows what day. When I surrendered to this project I gave over the calendar. I come to at my desk. George has long since been conked out by the door to the deck. I have been thinking that Galen is keeping vigil on the couch, but I see now that she isn't. I open the front door to call for her. George is too far-gone to notice. I yell her name, whistle and clap my hands. She doesn't come.

I go back inside through the bedroom door, get into bed with my coat on, lie there a moment, then get up again. I close the front door, heave George up from the floor and make him get excited about jumping up on the bed by thumping the bed while saying key dog vocabulary like "leash" and "walk." He complies and then looks surprised, a little disappointed but still good-natured when he realizes that the bed itself is the terminus. I lie down beside him, hold his paw, sleep.

The next day is the Monday before Christmas, which falls on Sunday this year. I spend the day skiing in search of Galen and then waiting for her to come home. I don't find her and she doesn't return.

The next day I go early to the grocery store. I have considered calling the animal shelter and the veterinarian, making signs that show a darkly reproduced photo of her, but this all seems inappropriate finally, as if she would be insulted if she knew about it. Galen is neither lost nor stolen, something tells me.

So I stand in the canned fruit and vegetable aisle, looking at the ten cans of mandarin oranges in the cart. I look at the grocery list. It does say "mandarin oranges," right under "t.p.," third on the list. But I'm pretty sure I meant one or two cans when I wrote it. I think about putting eight back but instead go down the aisle and put eight cans of green beans in with them. Abandoning myself to the pleasure of a decision finally made, I load up on succotash, tomatoes, and beets. I head for canned meat.

At the checkout the man looks at what I've put on the conveyor, counts, then passes the same can of beef stew over the scanner fifteen times. Everyone is loading up on food for Christmas, but I believe he betrays the slightest bit of surprise over the amount and kind of food I'm pulling out of my basket. It is more than even the orphanage will need to get through the next snow.

"My dog disappeared yesterday," I say to him. This is the checker with whom I have an acquaintanceship, having recognized in him a kinship between his and my desire not to be bothered, a commitment to getting on with the job without frivolities. Still, despite the connection (because?), he might not be interested in my dog's disappearance and he certainly wouldn't see it as explanation for the food. I'm not surprised at this; I don't see the connection either.

He flaps open a bag. A boy comes to help. I press on, stupidly.

"A border collie," I say. "Black and white. Her name is Galen."

"Oh," he says. He looks at me. In my mind I will him to ask the right questions. But if he ever did take notice, it wasn't for long. His own concerns lap across his face again. "Do you want to drive up?" he says.

I look at the ten bags of groceries. Then back at him. At least we have the satisfaction of sharing the knowledge that this is a stupid question.

"Where can I find empty boxes?" I ask. He tells me; I take the register tape with the numbers of my two carts and go out.

Back at the cabin, it takes two hours to clear all the books off the shelves on the wall outside the kitchen, put them in boxes in the dining room, and stack the cans alphabetically on the shelves. I am impressed enough with the order to call Father, the judge. No answer. I call my lawyer.

"Roger," I say, "Galen disappeared day before yesterday."

"Oh, sweetie," Roger says. "I'm sorry."

"There was a snow storm. I was working. I must have let her out in it. It didn't look that bad to me. She didn't come back. Do you think it could be that simple?"

"Well, Amelia," he says, "maybe she's roughing it in a cave somewhere, enjoying her freedom. Maybe dogs go off to winter camp there."

"What do you know about dogs in the Adirondacks?"

If I can rely on him for that kind of answer, anything is possible. I find myself not breathing out. I have been up here long enough that either I have forgotten about irony or it has taken over my life.

"Look, Amelia, I was in a conference," Roger says. "Do you want me to tell Donovan about the dog?"

"No," I say. "Don't tell Donovan anything. Don't tell him I just bought two hundred dollars-worth of cans. I don't think he'd be interested."

"Amelia, are you okay?"

"Yes, fine," I say. "How are the divorce papers?"

I had meant to invoke a business tone as a means of letting Roger know I'm not losing it, but the question comes out sounding like an inquiry into the health of the papers. I put my hand over the receiver to keep Roger from hearing me laugh. He has known me as mostly level-headed, even as a child, and he might not appreciate the form my humor is taking.

He misses both the implications and the laugh. He tells me everything is moving ahead smoothly. The house ought to sell soon and, even before the profit is shared with Donovan as agreed, there is no reason the divorce won't be final in a couple of weeks.

Dear Mom," I write, "my divorce will be final in a couple of weeks."

It is dark and I never have taken off my coat. I sit on the sofa, the stationery on a book on my knees. I read the sentence I've just written. I re-read it aloud, but the idea still doesn't attain reality. I write "Sold," bumping my pen across the embossed Stony Brook address at the top of the page, but that doesn't do it either.

It occurs to me that you would appreciate the humor of the divorce papers too.

If I asked you how they are, you would say, "About as well as can be expected." And then, when we'd stopped laughing enough, you'd add, "They got such a bad start in life."

Or you might say, "They're doing a little poorly, if you must know."

The imitation of the countrified, down-home woman by the slim, soft, well-spoken, genteel mother of mine is as funny to me as if your voice actually did warm the cold air of my living room.

You would be concerned over my stockpile of groceries, though. And you would go quite silent when I tell you about Galen. Then you would say in your own voice that you were sure Galen will come back. For a little while, I would believe you.

"Galen's gone," I write. "I don't believe she'll come back."

I fold up the letter and stick it in the woodstove. However true, it seems cruel to say that, even to a mother I haven't seen in twenty-seven years.

Chapter Five:

New Year's

D ear Mom, Galen has been gone a week today. George doesn't appear to miss her. I took her rug up from the floor near the woodstove yesterday."

Putting the pen down, I look at the neat stack of letters on my desk. The date on the top letter is December 13 and I have written every day for at least two weeks, so, if I were still dating the pages, this one would be after the 25th. I haven't been dating the letters since the one about Galen I burned, but that hasn't stopped Christmas from coming and going.

"Christmas has come and gone, and no Santa. I've always had a lot of respect for Christmas and I'm astonished that it could pass through without my knowledge—on its own recognizance like a jolly, trustworthy criminal."

I'm sitting at my desk. I wear long underwear, two pairs of socks, jeans, my father's navy blue v-neck pullover, the blue snowflake ski sweater and a bulky Aran sweater jacket. My writing hand is suspended an inch above the table and I have to compress layers of yarn to get anything written. My blue slippers over rag socks prevent massaging warmth into my toes. The heart of pine floor might as well be stony ground. A cool, skim milk block of sunlight freezes on my back and my face burns from the open fire in the woodstove across the room from me. To concentrate the heat I have closed the doors to both the kitchen and bedroom, but there is already a futility to this enterprise, and this is only December.

Walking across the room to look out the deck doors, I warm other parts of my body. The deck railing has a hump of snow on it and there are snowdrifts, bonzaied, against the posts at the corners. No garden, only a devastated black corn stalk staggering out of the snow sea beyond the deck. I don't know where George is, and, of course, Galen. If I smoked, I would now.

My breath freezes in ice crystals against the glass. I step back from the door.

I have told you I am astonished over Christmas' stealth, and I would be if I could muster up enough emotion to, but I can't and I can't write you this either. By now I have thoroughly conjured your warmth and softness enough to know you would be disturbed by the cool, angular turn my life took.

But I have not spared you the details of the breakup of my marriage. In the past week I have described how passion became need and then pain. Donovan was staying home most of the time by the fourth—last—year of our marriage, trying to write his novel. Actually, he spent most of the day at the beach and no longer gardened or cooked. He had taken up raging at me like, he said, his drunken father and I, though quite successful at the university, was sliding laterally into regular fits of weeping, which seemed like natural events, as unavoidable as squalls on the ocean; much like, Donovan informed me, his pill-taking mother's.

Finally I understood that Donovan's creativity was being expressed not in art but in voodoo, conjuring his dead parents to occupy our once-loving, warm bodies with their clay souls.

It was something of a dark miracle: I had never even met my in-laws. Yet I, like his mother, was incapable of loving:

a selfish, devouring cunt who was living off Donovan's vitality and not giving anything back.

Except my life, except my life. I offered, one marital night of the living dead, to lie in front of his car. But he was angry I would even think of obligating him so.

That phase ended and the next began wherein he had nightmares with obvious phallic content and phantom pains up his right arm which made it impossible to write. I could not save him; I was called for but could not help: my arms were cut off, my legs weakened. It was a doomed effort. He began to look elsewhere.

He came home at four in the morning once to tell me two women he'd met in the bar wanted him to go home with the two of them. He let me know he had resisted by virtue of his discipline—not because I deserved his loyalty, which of course I did not, whore that I was.

It wasn't my style to pursue other men while I was married, but Donovan believed my relationships with colleagues were necessarily suspect and there were times I considered acting on his faith. The truth was that I liked, admired and trusted men, and, if I could be said to depend on anyone, it was on them. But, though most of my time was spent in the company of men, no one seemed particularly interested in breaking the various matrimonial vows. Maybe, as mathematicians, we knew that the resulting permutations were not sufficiently predictable.

What was clear was that I could no longer depend on Protean Donovan, who was metamorphosing into a silky before my eyes. Now my adored husband, now a supernatural beast, he was rarely to be found in my bed.

Notice I call him a silky and not the more obvious comparison: the Jekyll & Hyde duo. I did not want to acknowledge how horrified I was.

By the end of the year, the symmetry was irretrievably lost. The constant sniping ended and silence began; the advertisements of infidelity ended and Donovan began to sell the product. He would come in as I was leaving for work, wearing yesterday's clothes and someone else's perfume. He slept all day; I never did.

There was the dense month holding the recognition that the worst had happened to us, what in our passion and pride we thought never could: we had fallen out of love. He moved out. I worked on more elaborate forms of my grief routine, finished spring semester and arranged for the summer off. Before I left, I filed for divorce and put the house on the market. Donovan agreed to live in it until it sold.

When we met for dinner the night before I came to the Adirondacks, we sat opposite each other on our booth benches, slumped over on our haunches, hapless.

"Donovan's and my divorce is uncontested," I write to you on what I am taking to be the day after Christmas. I have gone back to the desk. "Who could win the contest? What kind of jackpot is it when all you get is the relief of knowing the worst has already happened? Can they tie a big pink ribbon diagonally across that? By the time I left I didn't feel angry anymore. We hadn't rejected each other. Remember the Scottie dog magnets? Well, we were rump to rump. The magnetic poles: where indivisibility splits."

I am happy as I can be with this project, with its clear intentionality. I understand now that I have simply kept moving from the inertia of the initial repulsion. A few days ago I made another trip into town to improve my stock of cans, order a tank of oil and three cords of wood, and have the car radiator flushed and filled with pure anti-freeze. On the way back from town the man on the radio promised much more snow before the year's end. There has been one blizzard, but I am dissatisfied with just that, excited about even more snow, about the weight of frigid precipitation building somewhere in the sky, getting ready to murder the blue white sun. The car is covered with so much snow now—three? four? days later—it looks like a fastback igloo in the driveway. I mean to go all the way into this new extreme of solitude.

I put the pen down again. For two weeks these letters have given me surcease, but for the past few days they have been getting shorter and shorter. I look around the living room for other subjects. Would you be interested in the math problems with their nice wood ash covering at the end of my desk? Would I have to explain the jump method to drive to zero, or would you get it instinctively? What about the elementary premise in the section of the paper I was working on, that if R has an identity then every unitary cycle R-module is isomorphic to an R-module of the form R/J, where J is the left ideal of R? Does the fact I have navigated by the homological maps of algebra for ten years put me forever beyond your reach?

This line of questioning is starting to make me anxious, so I pass on to the next point of interest: the woodpile. It is a thing of beauty. I spent a day—it might have been that impish Christmas day—stacking three cords that had been delivered and then splitting a few days' supply. The split logs are symmetrical, stacked with admirable congruity next to the woodstove, the colors varying in each wedge from the dark brown of the bark to gold encircling the red isomorphic triangle of the core but varying predictably, evenly.

But, somehow, I acquire the conviction it would be better to hit you with one of the split logs than to impress upon you that your daughter split them. Same goes for the dirty pan sitting on top of the woodstove. At some point I have forsworn the use of the kitchen range and begun to use the woodstove. I don't wash anything anymore. I don't recall the last time I went into the kitchen.

You would not, after all, understand the radical failures of femininity.

Domestication has also taken a slight beating too when it comes to night habits. I note I have slept on the sofa at least once or twice: there is my sleeping bag open on it and a pillow. I appear to be wearing hat and gloves in bed these days; they are arranged for easy acquisition in the appropriate positions on the sofa. The peach cover has disappeared underneath.

But I have not disappeared: I see it in the glass of the deck door gazing out. While my householding skills—never more than barely adequate—deteriorated, I grew radiant. I am still thin but there is a lucidity to my skin, a purity in the blonde of my hair that wasn't there the last time I looked. It isn't as if I have gained anything; I just look clarified, like properly heated butter.

I look back at the desk. I have written barely half a page today, on what may be Boxing Day. You have been brought up to date on my divorce and this seems the limit of the discourse. I don't even write "Love, Amelia." I fold the letter into an airplane and sail it across the room. It lands delicately, just outside the cylinder of the trashcan.

On what may be the next day I go to the bathroom and check my underpants. Ordinarily altogether non-chaotic about my periods, I am puzzled that I am now at least two weeks late. I think about the girls in school who talked about having their menstrual cycle disappear when they were on a starvation diet. I suppose this is what has happened to me.

For instance, in the past twenty-four hours I can remember eating only a can of okra.

I zip my jeans and go look out the front door. Standing there I consider and reject the idea of snapping on the narrow skis for my dawn walk. As usual, I am up long before the sun is. I no longer think of Donovan in the morning. I am simply catapulted from the bed by something unnameable, a value I cannot assign.

Normally, I work on a letter while I wait for the day's lightening, but I didn't have anything to say today and so I have simply waited until it is light enough to ski. As the sun so to speak comes up, I realize I don't feel like going out: the air seems colder than usual, dense with the threat of snow, more like going into a walk-in freezer than going outside.

Besides I am less restless than usual. It is possible I'm even hungry. Maybe the self-help books have a point after all: once you have confronted your pain and accepted it, you are free of it. Do letters to my dead mother and the conviction that my divorce papers are moldering in the post office box constitute confrontation and acceptance?

I push open the door to the kitchen and am dazzled for a moment by the sweet, clear sunlight on the white appliances, table, walls. I rummage through the zipped locked bags of vegetables in the freezer and find some ham slices and a bagel underneath the big bag of frozen basil. I have faith that the eggs I find in the refrigerator are still with us. I take this bounty back to the living room and close the kitchen door again, a little relieved.

I toast the bagel by splitting it with the Swiss Army knife and laying its white skin face down on the stovetop. Eggs and ham join forces in the skillet that is so well seasoned from being unwashed it doesn't need additional butter.

But when they reach my plate their disintegration begins. For approximately two forkfuls and one bite of bagel, everything is fine. Then the mixture begins to look hostile. I give up on this possibility. Whatever made me think this could be appealing? I keep what I've eaten down and give the rest to George. Or rather, I put the plate on the deck for George or as a contribution to the outdoors at large if he doesn't come in time.

I am still not restless and, in fact, I feel rather calm. I might say beatific, if I were given to spirituality.

I am not, but I do give myself to the sofa and one of those popular books on physics. I sleep most of the day.

The next morning I wake up in my bed, dressed in the usual nighttime outfit: long underwear, rag socks, a flannel nightgown, wool hat and gloves. There is a dazzling day through the single bedroom window, shooting its own and snow-refracted light into the darkness of the log cave. I can see in the light it got so cold in my bedroom overnight the bottle of Oil of Olay on the dresser froze and broke. The puddle of pink and glass looks as jolly as everything else does this morning. I laugh, startling George who was sleeping along my flank. But, after a moment's hesitation, he is perfectly willing to wag his tail, remembered as a human remembers bike-riding.

"I feel, I feel," I say to him, "oh, blessed." It comes out like a sneeze. "I feel blessed."

I pile the blankets on top of me till the weight is satisfying and then I go instantly back to sleep.

"Dear Mom," I write, "I'm pregnant. You're the first one I've told. I haven't done a test, but I'm sure. When I lie with my hands on my belly, I feel filled with light. This may sound eerie—though maybe not to you, given where you are—but I hear the music of the spheres, a strange not entirely beautiful spinning humming half-human sound moving both forward and back.

"I must have gotten pregnant at Thanksgiving, so that makes it about five weeks, though the obstetrician would call that seven, counting from the last period. I don't know how I know this bit of practical math. An August baby, by my calculation."

I'm having a little trouble with this letter. It is the first I've written in nearly a week and I'm sticking a little.

I know I'm pregnant. I know I am eerily, transcendently satisfied. But I'm also frightened and more than a little reluctant. Except for the occasional nausea—and that is less, really, than from the emotional flu—my body feels splendid.

But this is, in itself, a problem. I feel occupied—actually possessed. I have been colonized, and I don't really like the feeling. My life will never belong to me again.

And, talk about problems, this all makes me feel much closer to you, but what does that mean when even I understand you're dead?

I give up on the letter and turn on the radio I've fetched out of the dining room. The classical station is on. I used to rock and roll; now it's Mozart. It is New Year's Eve. The business about the New Year's baby isn't lost on me.

It's morning and I stand at the closed but uncurtained deck door with Don Giovanni for company. I see neither George nor signs of him. I unbutton the button on my jeans. It may be my imagination, but it seems to me I'm already expanding. The sun warms the top layer of clothes so I open my ski sweater, take it off, and then remove the other layers: the V-neck navy blue sweater of my father, a tattered red flannel shirt, black turtleneck, heavy long underwear, and the little thermal t-shirt Donovan bit my nipples through. I put the ski sweater around my shoulders and let the sun stand on my clearly already increasing breasts. They are respectable now where once they were merely adequate, a non-hindrance. Now they are getting high and full, feeling like silk; the aureoles are expanding and darkening and even my warm nipples are erect. I hold them as if they are borrowed.

I haven't been out of my house for more than a week, but I have been growing more conscious lately of the presence of the white telephone nearly glowing next to the sofa. I don't quite expect someone to call, but I feel as if I might have that expectation soon.

Other than this slight, gray dread, I have spent most of the time in a state of butter-yellow contentment. I can't remember ever in my life feeling so softly and completely self-contained, a kind of loving invulnerability: serenity.

But my mind, underneath the drug of hormones, frets. There are technical problems. The baby is due in August: will it be born in time for me to get it started in life and then get back to work at the beginning of the semester? Will I

have a mathematically inclined child who arrives just when
it is supposed to? Or will Donovan's procrastinating genes
dominate?

And, speaking of Donovan, what would he say about
this child? I've put off even writing to you about this angle.
Sometimes one withholds a little, even from the dead.
Would Donovan be happy? Would he get a job and settle
into fatherhood? Would he give up floozing in exchange for
two in the morning feedings? Some men adjust to sudden
fatherhood, I understand.

I also understand my husband isn't one of them. His
happiness at the news would take the form of polishing off
several bottles of gin in celebration, significantly speeding
up the process he is only doggedly pursuing now. Until I
was pregnant I was not at all sure I wanted a child, and I
know for damn sure Donovan doesn't. He can no more give
up floozing than I can mathematics. He would see this as
the ultimate feminine betrayal — my fraudulent use of every
woman's trump card: her inevitable control of reproduction.
A kind of racketeering of fertility. No, this child would send
Donovan into an unimaginable rage such as I've never seen
him in before. He has relied on me to be tough, masculine,
to bar his random procreative urges with muscularity and
birth control. I had been too grateful at Thanksgiving to
think of it.

What would I tell this child about where its father was
five nights out of seven? Is drinking a job? And am I cut out
to be one of those women with child who is so clearly alone
with it, even with her husband beside her, who shows her
detachment with every gesture, with the way she holds her
chin? How am I supposed to tell Donovan's importuning
from the baby's? Would I be able to discriminate, choose the
right one?

Born, will she be as real as she is to me now? Because I
can see her now, our child. She is a girl, about four or five,
whose hair is blonde and cut in British bowl-style. She is

slightly tall for her age, more coltish than round. She wears a print sundress and stands in the surf, studying the effect of the incoming rush of water and its recession on her feet.

I am her mother, but somehow distant from her. I watch her from the steps of my gray, weathered beach house where I live alone in bleached-out, stonewashed light. Maybe someone else has been taking care of her all these years, but she is, anyway, mine, and I feel the pull in my belly that attaches me forever to her.

But I blink my eyes or look away down the beach for someone and when I look back she is gone as if she never stood there. She is certainly gone, but where? Up the beach and away? Did someone take her? Did she go into the surf?

I'm lying on the sofa when the vision ends, a little chilled from having stepped out of the sunlight, the tug in the muscles down my crotch pulling me back.

The vision continues into the first week of the new year, but as the days go by the sight of the little girl becomes less vivid and the time of her absence longer and longer. This is not a dream.

At the end of that week, I stand in the open front door at dawn and consider skiing. On all sides of me, the hot inside air rushes out, exchanging staleness for austerity. There was a thaw yesterday and overnight the snow has gotten an ice covering. My skis would twist out from under me. I go back inside and put on my hiking boots. George has been somewhere—the kitchen? Did he come in while I had the door open?—and joins me. We go out together.

I push my foot through the glaze and begin my walk, the aimlessness of which is its ritual. I find most of the time I can step through the ice, but I feel surprisingly lighter than usual. I suppose, despite the expansion, the child has not yet multiplied its cells maniacally enough to add to mass. In some places I skate and fall.

My golden retriever, despite his size, almost always skates on his uselessly massive pads. George, who before this winter was never vicious or a hunter, catches a scent and slips and runs after it. He disappears into the forest to my left, his high, excited hunting bark receding until the only sound left is my boot making muffled, regulated thunder as it goes through the ice.

I am no more careful about where I'm going now than I ever was. The relentlessness with which I choose the unfamiliar direction at every chance has always indicated to me a desire either to lose myself or to find something new. On skis one gets lost faster, but I never stayed lost.

It was something of a disappointment then. Before I realized I was pregnant I would have said, virtually free of the principle of uncertainty, that to lose myself would be an un-hoped-for blessing.

But this is almost certainly no longer the case.

Under the circumstances—a young career, a smashed marriage, a crippled psyche—many women would consider an abortion. But I have always found myself oddly seduced by life—not putting myself in the way of it intentionally but not unwilling to be carried forward by it if caught in a current, a rip tide. It is a weakness, the failure, ultimately, of discipline; how I will be diverted finally from a successful, arithmetic life. But there we are, washed away as irretrievably, as incorrectly as the way I love my sidelined husband—loving not just in spite of the flaw but because of it, charmed by accident.

And I have lost enough, I'm fairly sure. Mother, father, husband, dog, weight. A couple of days before, I put the radio back in the dining room. I had a bad moment when I realized that the phone was preternaturally silent and I picked it up to find no dial tone. But then that too became right and meet, what I had asked for really. I made one more trip into town for what I consider an adequate food supply for the winter. The oil in the furnace tank is probably half gone, but two and a half cords of wood still seem luxuriant. It means I can lose touch with humans altogether. I am confident I will find my way. My body, like anything else's in the woods, can take care of its own embryo. Prenatal care can wait.

I crash through the snow crust in a thick part of the woods. It is still early. The trees are so dense here I have no idea whether or not there is a sun up there today. I take my hat off and stuff it in a coat pocket. My hair feels heavy and free as I stomp with an exaggerated, knees-up stride, folklorically, from side to side: a hulk, a painted, non-hibernating member of the woods census.

I come out of the woods on the wild side of my mountain and look over toward the neighboring mountains. The pine trees over there are frozen in snow-encrusted attitudes as if perpetually blown by the north wind. It registers with me that for a couple of days I have felt oddly unpregnant. Add the loss of hormonal bliss to the list. I suppose the rest of the pregnancy will be simply uncomfortable. The first burst of good feeling must be nature's way of talking you out of abortion. I walk back into the woods.

George takes the responsibility for not losing touch with me. Soon he comes sliding back over the glaze, the animal he pursued having joined the conspiracy that makes all living things around us phantoms. He skitters comically for a moment, trying to stop himself, and bumps against my knee. I almost lose the balance I've found on the ice inside the forest.

I am watching a house.

The summer vacationers, perched in warm Manhattan apartments, know nothing of the lives their houses live in winter. I consider this a gift from heaven, a means of entertainment: my sense of realism has loosened up enough to allow a belief that this house looks back over the drifts under its windows, hunched in snow-protected relief until it is violated again by clumsy adults, racketing children, and summertime.

But I have made a mistake about this house. As I watch, a square, gray-haired man in a plaid jacket comes out into the dark early morning. He begins to cover the woodpile against the new promise of snow. He is too far away to hear George's snarl, but he looks around anyway before going back inside. Maybe there are wolves in these woods.

I stand absolutely still, hand on George's head, until I'm sure he won't come out again. A city slicker, I think, a stock broker who, underestimating the difficulties of winter here, came up to relax and get away for Christmas in a house that won't actually provide relaxation for another six months at best. I lift my hands, palm outward, toward the house.

I am pushing the man away. He is probably a hunter. For the entire summer I mistook every man I saw for Donovan. It is a measure of the grief already passed that I do not believe for a second this man is my lost husband.

B ack at the cabin, snow falling as I come in the front door, I shake off my coat and hair, throw the coat on the sofa pile, trusting the woodstove to dry it out before I lie on or under it next, stamp my boots, and rub George with a towel. I put wood in the stove, go into the kitchen to fill the kettle, and put that on top of the stove. When I straighten up, I begin to hum the Lucille song and dance a forward-sliding two-step, arms lifted to include an absent partner, toward the pantry shelves.

> *You picked a fine time to leave me, Lucille,*
> *With four hungry children and corn in the field.*
> *You picked a fine time to leave me, Lucille.*

I twirl under an upheld arm on the woman's name, end up facing the bookshelves, and consider whether to have corned beef hash or beef stew for breakfast. Although neither makes me nauseous, neither strikes me as appealing either.

I think of my seahorse-like child and decide on beef stew. Taking a can opener from the litter of utensils accumulated on the chest in front of the sofa, I open the can and dump it in the unwashed pan on a trivet on the stove. George is already asleep on his rug beside the stove.

Observing his oblivion to the empty space beside him, I realize I, too, have thought I could stand her absence, steeped as I've been in hormones. For a split second I'm suffocated by a sob jammed upwards in my throat as I imagine Galen there again, sleeping haunch-to-haunch with George as she always did.

The vision and its attendant sob dissolve as blindingly fast as they came. I squat down to rub George's gold head and then stand to stir the stew. I don't say anything to him, though I always would have before, all our lives together until this winter set in. He doesn't seem to miss the conversation any more than he misses Galen.

I lose as much as a week. Near the middle of January I have pains around what must be my left ovary. The pain frightens me enough to move the telephone next to the bed before I remember its connection has been cut off. I leave the phone on the nightstand anyway. All the people I would really want to talk to—whether dead or dead to me—can be reached by a silent phone. The pain stops and I sleep.

Late the next day there is a brown stain on my underpants. There is no pain at all for a long time. I consider lying down but put on my hiking boots and go for a walk instead.

It is almost dark when I come back to the house. I'm not sure where I've been. When I look behind me to see if I left a trail of red on the snow, there is only the gloomy iridescence of snow in the night.

Indoors, there is blood—a lot of it and quite an extraordinary color. Primary red, so bright it is almost a cartoon color. It comes out as if someone has inserted a clear glass tube—a beaker, something clinical—inside my uterus and simply let everything slide out.

It is strangely less frightening now it is here than when I was waiting for it, unsure it would come. This is simply an experience, albeit odd. Not only smooth blood comes out, clots do too. It requires one thing: the discipline of abandon, like falling backwards into a snowdrift to make a snow angel.

It is simply my duty not to get in its way.

George was on the walk through the woods with me but has now disappeared. He has done all a familiar could under the circumstances, or at least all he could. Galen might have had a wider range of possibilities, but she doesn't show. I circle the house inside, from kitchen to living room to bedroom and finally I open the dining room doors so I can pass through the chill. My mind is easily occupied with the zones of heat and cold, from Baja in the living room to Vancouver Island in the bedroom, breezing across the Kodiak Island dining room and the Prince Edward Island kitchen. I feed part of the mathematics problem to my head, but it refuses that, daunted finally. Even daunted by the possibility of getting more firewood. I hope I have enough to last through a spontaneous abortion.

It's lonely work, losing a baby, but, like having one I suppose, just has to be gotten on with. At first it seems surprising it can be done alone, but then I remember that everyone bears and loses alone, even with the room full of doctors, nurses, technicians, medical equipment, mothers, and husbands.

When the pain begins it is intense, white, epiphantic. But it somehow still excludes fear. I stop the circuit in the bedroom and lie down. Leaving my body in state on the bed, my mind drops down below the brilliance of the pain, crawling along in the tiny dim space beneath its barbed crystals. When I can, I go to the bathroom again. I leave more of my guts there. My face in the mirror looks right somehow, as white as it always was meant to be and beyond: the light of my skin is spiritual, beatified.

There is a coldness, a haughtiness, a pride one begins to feel about the pain, as if it could be beneath one, a member of a lower social order, trash. And there is the absolute loneliness. There is a desire to call someone, not from need of them but desire—not for company, which you know to be unobtainable—but for something social, no matter how superficial. A chat, maybe the suggestion of a future engagement. There is no answer, no dial tone even.

Because what is actually going on at the moment is that surely my own kidneys, spleen—whatever they may look like—heart are coming out too. But no; it's only the infinitesimal version of those organs, not real yet, only imagined, a potentiality in a body that isn't even frog-like and will soon be past.

Maybe what keeps the fear at bay, makes the pain an entity that doesn't entirely include me, is the sense—and this must be the definition of ephemeral—of accompaniment: a faint but vastly, strangely reassuring voice humming along, along with the pain, granting a small amount of consolation as it takes back what it has given. Or maybe it is just a spirit from the place that sent the child and to which she returns.

If I never before and never will have again any sense of metaphysical presence, then what I have to say about it is that it is entirely bittersweet, the purest irony I have ever known. It gives the greatest pleasure of one's life as it takes it away. If it is there when I die, I will follow it as a child's eyes follow the light, even as he or she ought to resist, cry out, to rage, until the illumination is utterly gone and the child with it.

The return of the pain is inevitable, the terrain of it endless. It is simply monotonous after a while, the grooves for it blasted into my cerebral cortex, what I will be doing the rest of my life. But finally, just as I think that this work, to which I seem horrendously suited, will kill me, a large clot is expelled in one mind-blasting, gut-grinding wrench.

What there was of me and of Donovan is gone, chromosomes down the toilet.

The pain, having accomplished its mission and being a sensible, pragmatic sort of pain, stops abruptly. I fall instantly asleep.

The next night I lie in the bathtub. The lure of the warm water is more powerful than dimly remembered warnings against this form of consolation, the seduction more persuasive than threats of infection. I am tearless. Turning out all the lights around the house, I have lit ten candles in the bathroom. Mozart's Dies Irae plays endlessly in my head.

Lying in the tub as if in a crypt, my body is my child's tomb; the bathtub is mine. I am burying us, the only way I am able.

White body. White water. White bathtub. Too clean.

We are all one now. You, my baby, me.

Miscarriage is common, I hear your voice tell me, something like twenty percent of first pregnancies. Most of the time, you explain, it is because there is something wrong with the conception.

By this I understand you mean there is a problem from the very first, in the genetic blueprint. Donovan and I fucked up again; we clashed, mismatched. When the embryo got to the fuck-up gene, it simply stopped growing.

It takes the uterus sometimes as much as a month to catch on that the embryo is no longer viable and then it expels the tissue.

Your voice sounds suspiciously doctorish, a little too biologically-oriented for the soft, ditzy woman I believe you to have been, but no matter; what you say is a comfort. What it boils down to is that it used to be a baby; now it is necrotic.

I have always been fond of transformation stories. The little mermaid who went from fish to human to surf, all for love. And the one about the girl who had to hand weave twelve coats from nettles and do it in complete silence for her twelve brothers who had been turned into swans. She did it, too, in the nick of time—just before they hung her as a witch for such silent, inexplicable work.

She did it for love of her brothers, to save them from permanent swanhood. Those two stories of miraculous, extravagant generosity—the mermaid's and the sister's—I can clearly remember your reading to me. Then there was a later childhood favorite of mine that was no classic, just a library book I discovered on my own and checked out so many times I could find it without the help of any adult or Dewey Decimal.

This anonymous, large-format text had to do with a mannequin in a store window that two children thought looked so much like their dead mother they made Christmas presents for her. When the children overcame their caretaker's resistance to the project if not her disbelief, they offered their gifts up to the glass of the window display. Then the children thought they saw a tear in the mannequin's blue plastic eye.

But I hadn't gotten the coats made in time; the mannequin never cried. And my baby was foam on the water; she was surf.

If the Snow Queen, coming out of her heartless ice kingdom, had given birth to the Little Mermaid it would have been the same thing: a blizzard over the ocean. Impressive at first, but as soon as the snow hit the water—pfft.

Steam, then nothing.

For a week I bleed. Then that is done. The day finally comes when I have not the slightest uterine cramp. I get dressed on this day and go with George on a short walk.

There has been more snow while I was inside. Weak, I can feel my strength coming back, a definition to my thigh muscles as they drive my leg and foot into the snow. I know by now that no infection will happen to me. My health is another slap in the face.

I walk a short distance down an old logging road, a discernible human trace under the frigid bower of snow-laced pines, a cold bride-alley. I go back along it.

When I get back to the cabin I sit down at my desk. I can already feel that soon I will be so restless I will have to walk or ski again, but for a moment I am not driven. Or not driven by physical restlessness.

I think for one nearly panicky moment that it is Maria I want—Maria's voice, her arms around me, the smell of her perfume, her meaningless, comforting promises that things will get better. But the wish clamps off before it hemorrhages.

I look at the stack of letters to you, beginning with the one mid-December, telling you of my plans to stay here, going through the loss of Galen and the beginning of the pregnancy. I have not written to you yet about the miscarriage.

You already know. A letter would be clumsy and redundant. I feel that you and I understand each other even better right now. We are sitting together in a quiet room. There is nothing more for us to do than pull the gauze curtain aside to look, occasionally, out the window.

But this raises another epistemological problem. If you know everything already, what was I doing with all these letters? And what do I do now?

The first ones, telling about college and graduate school and teaching and Donovan, had brought me the same sort of satisfaction I'd had as a child, recounting my life to her.

But the last ones, the short ones, irritate my hands. All the results of the past—the deeds, the feelings—are beginning to feel puny compared to the high white silence I'm coming into.

The letters are beginning to look like a senseless attempt to hang unconnected entities together in a dark web of significance.

The words themselves look like arbitrary black scratches on a pure white field which, though undisturbed by language, would plump up if left alone, would become more satisfied, like a pasture put to rest by snow.

I put the mass of paper in the stove without any further hesitation. Of course, the stove is where they belong, their mailbox.

On a scrap of paper I write:

> *Two things in the kitchen that we aren't sure what is in:*
> *—kitchen bouquet*
> *—Angostura bitters*

I drop the paper on the floor.

When I look up night has fallen. So this is the next step. If I am x and the day's passing is y, the frame of reference is now in motion, rotating.

CHAPTER SIX:

Epiphany

B y the time Adirondack winter has set in in earnest
and the aftermath of the miscarriage is completely
over, I have given up contact with the mathematics
department at Stony Brook, my father in Virginia, my lawyer
Roger, my estranged husband Donovan, my lost dog Galen,
and, very nearly, you, my dead mother.

I have even begun to lose touch with theoreticians
of whom I was once fond. For instance, Poincaré once
opened things up in my work. The questions he asked
were themselves illuminating. When he asserted that one
seeks the motion of a variable point (coordinates x, y and
t. where t is time) by giving the velocity as a function of
the coordinates, he raised the question of whether or not
the moving point describes a closed curve. Does it always
remain in the interior of a certain plane? He borrowed the
language of astronomy to ask whether the orbit of this point
is stable or unstable.

Good questions, Poincaré, I said once, and saved myself
a lot of useless theorizing.

But now he is my limit in every department.

I might have gotten some kind of handle on a personal
application of this abstraction, made a stab at a Poincaré
map of my life, except I've lost track of t altogether.

It disappeared somewhere in the last month, swept away or buried in the great deadening peace of ceaseless snowstorms. Now I know only this: the question of stability is ultimately undecidable.

So I sit on my couch, letting go of the sense of the day's passing, and then the week's. Or it is taken from me. The distinction is trivial.

I no longer walk. The snow has never stopped as long as I can remember and on some indistinguishable eddy of the sea of time I could no longer move through the drifts and stopped trying to.

The house is still. Wood pops excitedly over its consumption by fire, its destiny; mortar crumbles occasionally, cannonballing for the floor. It is quiet enough to hear the electrical wires hum, even through the shush of falling snow. They hum because they are compressed by the snow. Sometimes they fail. No one drives down my road, including me.

I closed off the bedroom at some point. I brought clothes out but never change what I have on, so they go into the pile I composed on the sofa. It is a welter, a color and texture extravaganza, inappropriate combinations of summer tennis whites and lizard cowboy boots, a bag lady's dryer-load.

The kitchen door stays closed, and I only go in there to forage. There is no need anymore for a separate refrigerator in there. It is so cold the white dishes and crystal glasses on the open shelves seem to have been additionally cleansed by it, a different kind of autoclave.

But the kitchen is too bright generally, so I retreat to the den of the log living room. Crouching by the stove sometimes and sometimes curling into the nest on the sofa, I keep the heavy curtains drawn over the sliding glass doors. For a while I watch the outdoors through the uselessly large summertime window in the front of the house. When the pine boughs have collected enough snow they look like dancers at a Virginia cotillion, stately and weighed down by their finery, men and women looking equally comic and dignified, about to whirl into a slow, graceful and gawky reel, twirling off their white linen and lace as they dance, then promenading off two by two all green again though still wintry, leaving the landscape blank and waiting for the next pavanne. Or maybe a cakewalk?

Finally I cover the window with a blanket. The room is infinitesimally warmer.

I notice the pantry shelves already look desolate. So I didn't plan the food supply carefully enough. I feel no horror over this. Having no intention of correcting it, I don't have any intention of dying either. I'm not sure what I mean by this.

With some mild form of relief I find I have neither anxiety nor hope over any of this. The embryo seems to have taken the meaningful future with it. This is sad but also obviates any real need for fretting. I simply note that I have eaten most of the vegetables and all of the fruit. It is barely a month past the winter solstice, not even halfway through the Adirondack winter.

Inside the laundry pile, my body has lost sensation, or refined it so it feels in only one place at a time. My mouth will have a sensation of hunger that excludes the discomfort of a boot toe stuck in my back. Sometimes my cunt will feel desire, but I cannot feel anything in my breasts at the same time. After a while the memory gets cut out and finally the touch itself seems not so much odious or inadequate—not noticeable enough to rate a negative number—but simply superfluous, unimportant, null set.

Then at some point wisps of thought about people begin to pass through with the substance and lazy speed of slight clouds at high altitudes.

I think about Maria and wonder if she has written to me or tried to call. I think about her offer to come interrupt me and realize I no longer feel even the perverse resentment of being rescued.

Then I begin to have thoughts that are not memories but visitations. I see Maria's gracious white farmhouse in the evening, one shade bluer than the snow on its lawn, the grape arbor a tangle of dead vines. I see the Bronco in the driveway and warmth and light inside the house. Maria greets intelligent, solid Leo. More people are arriving; the house seems remarkable to me for the way it lets people in and out. This may be a departmental function. Faces are distracted but composing themselves, getting ready for the pleasure of hot rum and sweet cakes; they are willing.

There are departmental children there who don't have enough on the plate of their life to be distracted, so they are more straightforwardly disgruntled over being there; some are eager for food. The snow has worn thin for them as entertainment and probably Maria has rented a video that portrays violence in comic form, the most successful recipe, as Maria well knows, for holding kids' attention.

I think about Maria and Leo's decision not to have children. What sort of decision is that? Does it have an essential nature? Is it against life? Does it, wisely, reflect one's acceptance of his or her limitations?

Why is it that I was never able to make those sensible choices, for a man who would stand by me stolidly, for the recognition of my limitations, fears, insecurities, need?

Why could I never see a warm, secure home as anything but a coffin? Why always the need to reach outside it, to link one number to the next, add, multiply, acquire another function, ride the magic carpet of exponentials, of some number to the nth?

Why was it that to let go of those risky choices—Donovan, babies—though I clearly did not have the wherewithal to actually succeed in the pursuit of them and the failure seemed to be thinning me—why did the relinquishment of these desires mean a cutting loose from life, making me a helium balloon floating free? Why did giving up on what was patently dangerous to me axiomatically mean I become disembodied, a spirit without even the satisfaction of being dead?

No matter. There we are.

Floating free at some point, high above Virginia some days, watching the Potomac River snake around the nation's capital, then leaving the river and sailing over the horse country around Warrenton and Culpeper, tracing Route 29 South through countryside that looks from my height like an animated map, until finally one day I come closer to the Blue Ridge, those bosomy blue hills that will always mean home, their great consolation their haunting natural beauty, saying accept this peace, stay, rest here.

Which I do, hovering in tiny eddies of wind above my grandmother's house, then dropping quickly down to the window of my father's study, the only lit room in the house.

Did he celebrate Christmas? Did he try to call me? Does he wonder where I am, what I am doing? Does he speculate about the nature of the problems in the papers I am ostensibly writing? What could he possibly say if I told him his only grandchild had returned to the sea?

I enter the room where he is reading in an armchair, the one lit lamp in the house a shaded one on the table next to him. He is not actually reading, I see. His chin is propped in the crotch of his hand between thumb and forefinger.

His eyes are closed, the tired blue folds of skin at rest around them, although his eyes move under the lids.

He may be dreaming of her, but what do I mean by her? His mother? His daughter? No, of course not. Of my mother, of Snow White. Of coming to you soon, Ma.

I rest my phantom face against his, my tired blue eyes closed beside his identical blue eyes closed. We have had our grief, we two. There is no call to torment ourselves any longer; we may let go now. Release.

I float away from my resting father, into the house and up the long dark stairs, walnut and night, past the luminous white curved railing that makes an indoor gallery of the upstairs, then swirl toward my grandmother's room at the sharp end of the curve. I would resist this if I could, but not after I see it.

My grandmother's body lies in marble peace on her bed where, under a carpet of growing flowers—white alyssum, purple phlox, jewel moss roses—she has the only pleasure she will ever have: she has sovereignty. Life is, at long last, irretrievable.

The winds sweep me away from her triumph and fling me back around the curve, past my childhood room where I sit on the edge of the bed, forever fourteen and stunned, permanently confused, plowed under by hope and suspicion. I want there to be something I can say to this girl, but there is nothing. I throw myself to the winds and am gone.

Back to the cabin where I find myself crouched next to the stove, my hands on its black side, willing myself back into this body, through burns if need be. But of course I'm not that loony, or not yet anyway. The fire is out.

I build another one, using the last of a July newspaper, some pages from an early draft of the mathematics paper, kindling and logs piled haphazardly around the stove amid a pool of bark and wood chips. I have dropped farther and farther behind in the race for a Betty Crocker Homemaker Award. Once the flames have acquired a life of their own and encouraged the reptilian blood in my toes and fingers to move along again, become mammalian, I sit down at the desk to consider the issue of looniness.

It is possible I am or will be. Possible, though not, in my opinion, inevitable. There is no out-and-out insanity in my family, only rampant eccentricity.

My grandmother, denim-jumpered and wispy white-haired, moving her low canvas camp stool from iris bed to rock garden, gnarled, powerful hands coaxing weeds out of, life into her black Virginia dirt, her back turned rigorously to her lovely neglected home and all the human life inside it, could never be mistaken for a happy woman. You, Ma, imaginative and frightened, clinging to your child as to a spar in the hostile waters of the Oedipal sea, were a lovely, neurotic woman while you lived. My father is locked in the emotional Iron Maiden of having lost all the battles by forfeit, the only one of which he had a chance of winning the one he lost first: to simply live the rest of his life as a small man in the presence of a lovely woman; a man who, by grace, had received the blessing of the warmth in a wife he had been deprived of in a mother, and who lost it and who then accepted the inevitability of his deprivation.

But none of them nuts.

I don't know about previous generations—insanity seems to have been more acceptable or disguised in earlier times—so I don't have a complete set of statistics and can't say definitively I won't go bonkers. But I don't imagine I will.

I will go as far as I can, though. I owe that much to us all. So far I've gained a modicum of peace and that seems some kind of significant motion in a situation where all future tides threatened to be neap.

I eat a slice of corned beef from an open can. That is enough for now, whenever it is.

I don't need food anymore than I need a sense of time. My body has become honed, as a wild animal's will, by the discipline of winter. It may be possible a body can be taught to desire only what is available. If I walked on all fours, my belly, taut and empty, would curve upwards, like a female wolf's, between my pelvic bones.

At that time or maybe later I go to the front door and open it. It is so dark it must be night, although I haven't a clue whether it is the beginning or the end of one. The snow tonight is a little wet so it falls hissing. I step out from under the eave of the house and let the snow fall on my face, cooling my forehead and eyes.

As the dry fever of being indoors comes down, I realize I don't know where George is and I have no way of judging when I last saw him. I shrink farther into my skin and realize I cannot see any distance into the pines. I lose faith in my voice and in his response if I tried to call him. I fear the results of an attempt.

I stand in the dim light thrown out the door by the one lit lamp inside the cabin, letting the hiss cool me farther and farther down until I can feel myself contract and separate from the material body, then, small, float gently away to where I see George gambol cheerfully—nevermind the cold or dark or wet—up to the blacker hole of a cave entrance.

It is Galen's cave. She has collected pine boughs, rags, and someone's old lavender silk comforter—or maybe it wasn't old when she found it airing on a clothesline—to drag into the hole, upwards five or six feet, around a dogleg and into the den where she has made her finds into what must be called a sumptuous bed. There are bones lying about on the floor of large and small animals who in giving up their lives have prolonged Galen's. She is an efficient hunter and kills only what she needs to live, as if she had never known excess Alpo. Her coat is much dirtier than when I bathed and brushed it, but it is magnificently full, the proper raiment of a Scottish outdoor dog in winter.

George crawls on his belly up the tunnel and around the corner. Galen waits for him on her bed, head and ears up at first in alarm and then, as his scent reaches her, with a languid wag of her plume tail. He deposits his offerings in front of her, cooked sweet potato skins he has scavenged from someone's garbage he has had to go near to town to find. They eat together; George lets her have most of the skins. I do still fill his bowl on the deck.

When they have eaten George rests for a little while with his head in Galen's tail while she sleeps the divine sleep of queens on her bed.

George envies her the twitches moving her sleeping body—those of the hunt, no longer those of the anxious relationship of dog to human. He envies her finding what she wanted, her refusal to compromise. He understands that her love and loyalty and disappointment over Donovan could not be transferred correspondingly to Amelia, to me. She had to obey the constant high white whistle all dogs hear, calling them back to their basic nature whenever pain or sickness or the desire to breed overwhelms the cushy allure, the seduction of domesticity.

He understands her choice, yet must obey his own. He does not sleep there. His heart stays forever lodged with Galen in her den, but his soul—more than his duty: his calling, his vocation—sends him back into the forest at the foot of the stony hillside into which Galen has dug. He looks back once in the crepuscular light of dawn which is itself cold, steely, at the hill, snow covered except the flat sides of rock projections and the vertical strokes of tree skeletons, into which the hole of Galen's cave has already disappeared. He turns and goes into the dark forest where he may or may not lose his way, but he has no real choice. He will risk it, die trying to get back to me.

I very nearly see a golden shaft shooting past the snow barrows of what used to be the garden. The steely patina of dawn has indeed reached the cabin but no beam of sunlight, no George. I recollect myself.

I'm soaking wet. I go inside and stand beside the hot stove to towel off my face, hair, and clothes. I don't take off the clothes; I just let the Shetland wool of Father's sweater diffuse the water across its surface as it must have done for the sheep before they gave it up for my father. These clothes are the same ones I've had on since I don't know when: the thermal t-shirt, then the beige long underwear, rag socks, black wool turtleneck, red flannel shirt, two sweaters, one of which is my father's. Down below I see the square toe projection of my ski shoes and consider this novel. I wouldn't think of changing them. The entire outfit has come to feel and smell just right. It smells of my own odor plus a little of what I remember as Donovan's, a potent perfume of sweat and sex.

I climb back into the nest on the sofa to warm up and finish drying.

Some other time I get out for a minute and improve the bed composition by hunting for and adding Galen's old rug and my sleeping bag completely unzipped. These turn out to be a significant improvement and I feel my body heat will probably reach an adequate level as long as I'm in there, which is more than I can say for when I'm out of the nest. Because at some time or another it became clear to me I don't have enough calories to burn to keep me upright. My menstrual cycle, quite naturally, never did restart; now the culprit is clearly the fact that there is not enough fat on my body to keep feminine production going.

I sleep or doze or whatever it is I do when my mind is neither conscious nor having visions, travelling. This is a soggy state, one as far removed from hard integers as it possibly could be, way out in the calculus of abstractions.

Not only are there no numbers, there are not even any forms: no triangles, no pyramids, no tetrahedrons. It is like resting in a gray winter cloud—as peaceful, as cool, as damp, as oppressive and as sickening as that.

But there is no more sense fighting it than in a dirt-entombed corpse's trying to call its cells back together as they return to the earth not willfully or maliciously but with such infinitesimal irresistibility that the solid, immovable object finally switches its loyalty, goes over to the other side and joins in with its enemy so the battle is won by tininess, and the body, without moving, disintegrates.

I am coming, too, Ma. Sooner or later.

There is something wrong with the room: it is unnaturally full of light. What's more, I see as I come more and more into it, it isn't my room, not my cabin, not my icy mountains.

It's not even winter.

I am outdoors in Virginia in summer. I stand on the side of a lake on a grass bank at the foot of an emerald mountain and watch children play on a beach a little farther around the ellipse of the lake from me.

There is one little girl climbing the ladder to the diving board. She has a cloud of fine blonde hair haphazardly curling around her head and wears a sapphire blue bathing suit with a green flounce where her hips will be. She passes the opening to the low board and keeps climbing.

There is something about her awkwardness, enough fat still on her forearms and calves to interfere with smooth upward monkey movement, that indicates she is still very young, pre-school, a kindergartner at most. Someone should stop her.

But I see no one, no dark-haired older woman serene and blooming among the confusion of children and towels. Not even one tense over safety and lost beach objects. No mothers at all. So the child keeps climbing.

When she gets to the high board she clambers awkwardly over the lip of it and for a second I'm afraid she is going to take a dive for the sand. But she makes it in that miraculous way children accomplish stunts of which they are not capable.

She stops for a moment once she gets onto the plank and holds onto the ladder with both hands. She may finally be afraid now, afraid both to jump and to go back down. She is very high above the opaque brown-green water.

But then I see she is leaning on the ladder in order to lift her feet in pleasure. She turns to face out toward the water, releasing her hold, continues to pick up one fat-toed foot and then the other, dancing, anticipating and rehearsing the pleasure her feet are about to have flying out along the plank and then, pushing up a little at the end, going free. Obedient for a second not even to gravity.

The girl suddenly breaks out of practicing and races out. She flings her arms out and opens her mouth. No sound comes out, but there is a radiance of pure pleasure coming from every part of her body, from her chubby kneecaps. She tosses herself off the end: abandonment.

There seems to be some information in this for me. Did my child do this? Race out of my body down the red pathway, splash into the toilet but gleefully, knowing something I don't know: she can swim, she'll be back?

And who was I to stand in her way? I was only her environment, the stage for her experiment. Could the air have stopped the girl? Could the diving board have risen up against her pleasure?

A great, gray contentment settles into my living room after this. The loss of the baby is no less sad to me, but it has lost its particularity. It is sad but only to me; on another plane perhaps it has a purpose I cannot comprehend but is just the same, outside my will or collusion or knowledge. The possibility cradles me.

D ays have passed while I rested in the net of this sad consolation. When I come to, the call of the flesh has risen to a murmur and I find myself dining on a camper's dinner of warmed spaghetti, pork and beans, and cold apricots. I find this a tiny miracle of discrimination. What's more, the foods are neatly arranged on a plate that doesn't appear to be encrusted and the fork has nothing previous stuck between its tines.

At first I am surprised and delighted at the appearance of the food—both its presence and its arrangement—but when I put apricot to lips, I find it has all the flavor of a dream fruit. The spaghetti has no flavor either and, though pasta might naturally not taste like much, the pork and beans lack both taste and texture when put into my mouth. The food altogether has all the gustatory pleasure of an imaginary meal. I put the plate outside for George or whomever.

With food out, it is time to think again about where I've been and where I am. I try causing the visions; I ask for one of

Roger. But this is not vouchsafed. Roger, it appears, doesn't have the necessary fuel, the right mix of liquid oxygen and hydrogen, to power into my imagination. So, along with food, volition is out. Where I'm going will have to wait for more lucidity and curiosity than I can muster now.

The diminishment of food both in supply and demand and the attendant dwindling of my body do not impress me. The travelling and the visions strike me as perfectly credible and, more, comfortable.

So there's nothing to worry about, at least within my own number system. I do not intend it, but if my material being dispersed now I would be neither surprised nor alarmed. There are natural processes, after all; there are axioms. Girl plus care does not equal girl minus care.

But what I am beginning to be impressed by, I find, is the silence in my living room. At some point it has changed from a soft-edged, billowing spirit filling the room gently and benignly to its sister, a starker presence: the absence of sound. Over the next period of time when the absence sweeps into the room, it cuts the dustballs out of the corners of the room. It makes my eyes so dry they sting when I blink. When it sweeps through, I sit bolt upright on the sofa.

I am watching this presence one day, as if it were a scirocco and I a Bedouin who must get to know this enemy, though it shows no signs of intentionality. Still, enemy it is: recognize its power or die.

Without any warning, in a silent attack, I can see the other woman in the swirl of sand: Donovan's lover. On the other side of the hot grainy wind she sleeps in Donovan's arms.

She is small and dark, exotic. She is not young; she is at least Donovan's and my age. He has desired someone who could take care of him not less well than I could. She is at rest in his arms because this is where she wants to be. Though she is no artist herself, she loves his poetic soul.

They have gone to bed drunk on champagne and made love every way they can. When he holds her like this, her back against his chest, she can tell he is holding her and not holding her body as a shield against the memory of his chilly wife about whom he finally confessed after Thanksgiving, after the woman had spoken to the wife on the phone. The wife had sounded kind and cultured. Her tone had not struck the woman as odd, utterly out of place, until she was herself well into her own impassioned outburst against Donovan's stupidity in not explaining the situation, in giving her the wife's cabin phone number.

It had been easy enough for him to mystify his married state; he had only not to mention it. The wife is and always has been conspicuously absent from this house on the beach. In the welter of Donovan's life, no sign or scent of the wife is distinguishable, not in the kitchen, the yard, the medicine cabinet.

One day after Thanksgiving Donovan got himself together enough to sign the divorce papers, and the woman went with him to the post office to mail them to the wife whose first name on the envelope is Amelia and whose last name is not Donovan's. The woman has not heard and doesn't ask if Amelia ever signed and sent them back.

Partly, she doesn't want to interfere. She is quiet, self-sufficient, and this is some of what Donovan loves in her. Partly, to ask would create implications she doesn't hold with.

She is a teacher; she has her desires. She also understands that people are who they are. Before Thanksgiving she might have had some illusions about Donovan—did talent not sometimes lead to riches?—but after the holiday she knew that Donovan would give to her only insofar as he desires.

She wakes up the rest of the way, strokes Donovan's flank, and gets up. Putting on a petite-size white silk kimono, she goes to the kitchen and makes coffee.

On her way to the bathroom she stops by sleeping Donovan and stands over him sipping coffee. If she smokes, she will smoke now.

She watches his large, loving body twitch though a nightmare. She knows he knows even in sleep that she has left him.

Unlike me, she will not give in and get back into bed with him. She is strong and does not think, as I, even refrigerated, imagine: one must atone for the sin of ever thinking oneself separate: there are exigencies of the community, of the pack, making the role of helpmate not a social function that can be turned off and on but, no matter how old-fashioned, fundamental to survival. She does not show this kind of sympathy, which may well lack mercy. Or else this woman can discriminate better than I; she simply knows that this is not her mate.

She showers and dresses, then watches him a while longer. He will never give her a house or children or security. And she wants these things. She will have to look elsewhere, sooner or later. She leans over him and kisses his forehead. She smoothes the tangled black hair, oily from unwashing, sweaty from sex and the fever of dreams, back from his eyes.

"I have to go now," she tells sleeping Donovan, though he cannot hear her from deep inside the bony cavern of his nightmare. "Poor Donovan," she says.

She taps out of the bedroom and the house on sharp black heels.

Outside, a sandstorm blasts up and smothers us all. I sleep. Just before I tip over the edge, I think, Oh, my God, have I made up an awful lot of bullshit?

Something about the last vision has made my sleep spongy and, though I am sucked into it frequently enough, I am also ejected into small air pockets too, waking hundreds of times over the next few days. Finally, I wake up and stay there.

I have a fleeting desire to know what day it is, but even if I could find a calendar in my cobweb-festooned pile of papers, how could I figure it out? Ordinarily, one would have to know what day it had been and then have a guess as to how long it has been since then, both forms of knowledge that have forsaken me, or we have given up on each other.

How else could I figure it out? If I follow Poincare's lead into astronomy, could we figure out where I am by triangulation? For that, though, we would need to know two of the three points and what those might be in my case is pretty unclear.

I am standing at the glass deck doors, once more uncurtained, looking out into what may be an afternoon. The sky is close and getting ready to drop snow or night onto my house. I am sorry now I have never learned how to read the heavens. The only sign systems I understand are maps to territory that doesn't exist. If I accept my living room as one stable point—it does seem pretty much the same in location at least, although occupied by less stable entities and meteorological phenomena—what can I use for the other stable point? My mind? Nope, couldn't count on that. Though it is doing some pretty interesting new tricks, it would be hard to say they have stability as a conspicuous factor.

So let it go. Let it all go. Let the face in the glass be a wraith, the crystal-covered, bloodless reflection more real finally than the flesh. I have arrived now at a state of almost complete emotionlessness. This is what people call peace.

But it is more perfect than peace. It is empty, but there are no regrets over its emptiness; regret would count, be a positive number. And that is what I am empty of. Nirvana, then, is absolute zero. I am very close to it.

But, in thinking about looking for a calendar, I've gotten close enough to the desk to pick up a scrap of paper. I find a pencil too and my hand still knows it.

Sitting at the desk, I write in pencil a word my mother would enjoy: "contumely." I squeeze commentary into the fragment of margin: "Is it ever anything but 'heaped'?"

I drop that one on the floor and tear off a couple more pieces of paper. On one I write, "Of what is the famous tar one gets knocked out of one composed?"

I write quite a collection that day and the next. None is a mathematical notation. ("To meap means not to speak up for yourself. Do you often catch yourself meaping?") I do not sleep. After a while the scraps of paper accumulate on the floor, drifting, my own drunken boats, when the crack under the front door lets in the cold wind.

The pieces of paper curl from heat near the woodstove, from cold near the walls. When George comes in or I walk through the room the scraps sail in different patterns, a regatta without a goal.

Although I am cold and food still holds no fascination for me, there is something secure about the reduction my life has gone through. The littered room is as familiar to me as if I'd spent my earliest wild childhood in it: the gay disorder on the sofa; the soot covered lampshade; the bony desk and its cobwebbed ladderback chair; the darkly Indian-patterned blanket over the window; my clothes as smelly and comfortable as a pelt.

I try some reconstructions. As far as I can recollect, George began prowling on his own almost as soon as I stopped walking. He may have waited half a day to see if it was really true I had given up on the cold and airy sympathy of the outdoors. Although he always comes back, he is most often gone. He must have learned to hunt successfully at some point because, though thinner, he does not have the collapsed belly I have.

Once I have begun the sailboats I am aware enough to know that he is gone sometimes for days in a row. I go to the door if I notice when the grays shift into black, but, like the night of the Galen vision, I never call him. When he comes back, he scratches at the door; I open it; we go to our separate places in the room.

At some point after the scirocco, the visions slow down, become indistinguishable from dreams, then stop. About that time George begins to stay home more, leaving massive melted snow and mud prints on the boats. When he is indoors, he growls at the house noises—wood giving up its integrity to fire, mortar giving up its longheld place between logs, mice and squirrels scrabbling the uninhabited upstairs and occasionally in the abandoned bedroom.

Once when he is inside with me, the snow falls from the roof in a series of soft bumps. George charges the door, teeth bared, hair on his back up. After a few minutes and no invasion, he comes back to me on the couch, sniffs the part of my head that is not buried under the collage, and drops with a grunt to the floor. His head comes up, ears forward, when the next avalanche comes, but he stays down. His growls die out in time.

We are waiting, me and George. We are not sure what for.

I for one have achieved the peace that is a void and am reluctant to face the next step. Am I to be released now? Will the logic that has kept me together—my marrow producing red blood cells, my spleen and kidneys and liver and pancreas performing clean-up operations, letting my ovaries rest, firing the brain and the heart, keeping my eyes blue—finally give up its supremacy and let them all go? I do not know.

George, for his part, is angry about whatever it is that's coming.

Chapter Seven:

Valentine's Day

Wish *fulfillment is never what you wanted it to be.*
I write this to my mother and throw it on the floor. Blobs of paper are stuck here and there on the wide pine planks. Both George and I are responsible for the soggy footprints.

I don't want to be. If it were entirely up to me I would stay inside much more often. To tell you the truth, I want to go back to zero.

But mathematics collides with economics. And you have to grant Marx this point: idealism is a wonderful thing, but materiality cannot be altogether ignored.

I am reluctant to grant it; I wish I could claw my way out of flesh if it will not cooperate and simply become permeable, then thinner, then go. I try occasionally, scratching in the pale dry vein-reliefed back of my hand—not too hard but enough to leave chalky trails. Epidermis may give way; dermis has a will.

So, too bad for me. Being in a body can't be helped at the moment. I have collided with the inescapable, ironic property that says subtracting a negative number results in a positive one. I am, however hesitatingly and complainingly, adding up to something again.

This is all too clear to me the morning I wake up knowing not only it is morning but also February. The appropriateness of waking in the morning shocks me. I close my eyes firmly, with discipline. But they insist on flying open again.

The problem is the sun is rising. Don't ask me how my eyes know this: my back is to the window, plus the window is still covered by the blanket. Yet, the sun is rising and I know it. I can feel it, through the window, the blanket, Galen's rug, the sleeping bag, and my wardrobe. Warm rays, particles of solar energy nosing through the layers like airs, like the fingers of polite children into their Saturday morning parents.

I want beets. Purple, tender, a little salty. What I wouldn't give for a pat of butter. I push aside the covers and sit up on the couch. George, on the floor next to me, between the couch and the chest, whines from under the laundry that has fallen on him. He senses a change and doesn't like it or at least has some doubts. I get up and peek out the window, confirming. Icicles of brilliant light stab my cave-accustomed eyes.

I end up too blind to see if there are any beets left on the pantry shelves. I get back in the nest and pull it over my head.

"Don't like it either," I say from under there, "but can't make it go back down." I am as grumpy, as petulant as any child woken too early.

I hear George thump his tail where it is confined between the couch and floor. Shaking off the clothes as he stands up, he puts his front paws on the edge of the sofa and stands over me. I look out and rub his head. I scratch him between the eyes and rub his short snout. Finally I pull my other arm out and scratch him behind both ears.

"Phew," I say to him. "Gamey."

Nothing could be a higher compliment. A wriggle goes all the way down his spine and out his tail.

"No doubt I compete," I say.

He jumps down and turns several circles in pursuit of his hindquarters as if even the memory of a flea biting his tail were not ludicrous in this cold. He ends up facing the door and recognizes the need to scratch on it. He does so.

He glances back at me. He looks at the door, at me. He picks up his paws though he doesn't scratch again. Something—my voice? the head rub?—has changed his mind about the desirability of this new situation and he is thrilled again, the old George for whom companionship was the moon and stars. I get up and open the door.

Sure enough, sun sparkles on the snow weighting down the arms of the pine trees. None of it is melting; not even the air is warmed by the sun. But there is no question that the sun means to come back, that the solstice is long past and the vernal equinox inevitable. I shade my eyes.

George is already at the perimeter of our clearing. He stops and looks back, looking an invitation.

What the heck. I look down at my body. My suspicions are confirmed: I've been sleeping in even my coat lately. Hat and gloves are in the pocket. The ski shoes are, of course, still on. And the skis are still leaning against the house next to the door. I snap them on the hard projection out of the soft black leather of the shoes.

Although I have taken a couple of walks around the outside of the cabin lately, this is the first time I've tried skiing since before the miscarriage. As I reach the woods I realize the snow is very nearly too deep, but it is powdery, not slick, so I think I can manage it.

I move very cautiously at first, testing the snow and, more, my legs. There is a wobble there, a lack of geometry in the angle between the straight ski and my leg. I regret for a moment the uncertainty that comes with the freedom of my heel from the ski. But then my leg remembers; the muscles slide into place, bone and ligament cooperate. I begin to move on heaven knows what energy, surging out from the tight muscles in my ass upwards through swinging arms, downwards through stroking legs.

George is galumphing ahead of me. He turns back and gets down on his forepaws in dog-play invitation. He barks at my awkwardness, and dashes off, snow flinging from his chin and paws.

I pick up speed. In no time we are deep in the forest, me racing stroke by stroke, George at a full run beside me. Sun splashes on us in less dense spots and pours over us, flashing on George's golden coat, as we come out suddenly at someone's bowl-shaped field. We dive under the fence recklessly and leave tufts of hair and coat on the barbs.

We zoom like crazy around the rim with more speed than we ever could in the woods, my arms and poles and legs and skis swishing with so much vigor that, along with George's occasional high bark, our ruckus sends the herd of black angus hustling ungracefully down into the bottom of the bowl. We exit arbitrarily at another vector.

A little later we pop out of the woods into a suburb and I scramble to turn my skis around and get back into the woods. I am panicked by anything other than the occasional empty cabin of the summer inhabitant and the forest primeval.

At some point I sing, completely inappropriately to the season, "This summer I went swimming, this summer I might have drowned. But I held my breath and kicked my feet and moved my arms around."

Once, I wave my poles above my head while my legs keep their gliding stroking rhythm going forward. "I am lonely, lonely, I am best so," I call out triumphantly. George leaps up for the poles, playing a vertical game of fetch. I don't pay any attention when the sun rises into the higher haze and the snow begins again.

Finally I end up miraculously back at the cabin. George has been with me the whole time. We are both panting and tired. I am euphoric.

I stop by the ancient maple on the edge of my clearing and lean against it on one outstretched arm to catch my breath. George flops in the snow next to the tree and licks at the trickle of sap on its side, thinking it is melted snow. He is disappointed but not too badly.

I think about how the bark must feel on George's tongue and instantly the wood asserts itself against my hand. Even through the black leather of my glove, it feels marvelous. It feels like it is moving with life but in a solid and dependable way.

I take off my gloves and hold the tree on either side, pushing to make impressions of the bark on my palms. I may be imagining all this; it feels to me as if the tree has air arms that hold me, and its trunk beats warmth out to me without benefit of fire. I am hugging the tree and it is pumping life and warmth and energy through the thick wool of my coat just like it is pumping sap. The marks of the bark on my palms are irregular, gnarled indentations of dark blood; they are good, substantial, real.

I take out my Swiss army knife and carve "Amelia + Donovan" lightly across the trees crevices. I believe this to be a return of the favor the tree did for me, a sign not so much of love as simple presence that will eventually retreat into the wood's memory as my skin will forget its indentations while a brain cell retains their tracings.

As to the sentiment behind the sign, I do not actually believe Donovan and I could have stayed together or even that I wanted us to. I carve it out of some more general hope that pleasure endures, does not alter or disappear so arbitrarily or so absolutely.

Not on this earth perhaps but on some other planet, just at this particular moment, Donovan and I have never fallen out of love.

And this is not the end of my hopefulness.

I wake up in the morning again on what I'm pretty sure is the next day and—I'm not kidding—bounce off the sofa. I pull the blanket off the window. George is already outside, I guess. I go to the front door and call him. He comes. I'm astonished that this process, once wholly routine and then wholly moribund, can be recalled from the dead. I'm still dressed, even to the coat and shoes, so I step outside to join him in the gray morning rather than call him into the cave.

There is no sun today, but it is not snowing. I survey the pile of wood and count it as still substantial, probably three-quarters of a cord left. There has been activity at the splitting stump all winter. The driftwood gray of its upturned surface is free of snow and shows golden or brown wounds where the axe accidentally sank into it at different times. There are chips all around the stump, some fresh-cut and on the surface, others buried at various depths of the trampled snow around it. I assume it was I who did this, but I don't remember.

I must have used up whatever energy I had the day before, though, because I can't get the axe out of the stump this morning.

No matter. I take a couple of smaller logs inside unsplit and shove them in the stove. I can't quite remember what I should do with the cocks in the stove door. I have done this perfectly well without awareness and feel now strictly cursed by its return. I wonder not for the first time in my life how any of our instincts survive self-consciousness. I make a guess that the cocks should be about half open.

I get up from my knees and go out the deck door.

The snow on the deck seems to have been wholly undisturbed all winter. I duck to avoid icicles hanging from the roof. I slog across the deck and down the steps.

Not even a corn stalk marks the snow-sunk garden anymore. I scuff the snow where I think it might have been. Then I shovel with the square toe of my ski shoe. About a foot down I hit black dirt. Though it is only about three inches across and cold, as soon as I turn it over an overwhelming smell of rotting matter slams into my face. It is so strong at first that it is almost sickening, but then my nose gets accustomed to the strangeness, the redolence of something other than myself, and sucks in its sweet dark promise as if I could dine on it, grow as strong and straight and luscious as a leek.

But back inside I see the logs have not caught. I plunge into despair. I wonder how I ever thought they would: unsplit, the cocks half-closed. Probably didn't even open the flu. I put on my ski gloves and pull both logs out, then throw them, charred, out the front door. I follow them and snap on my skis. I am rising and falling this morning as if I were eating a dozen doughnuts.

Birds sing. I don't know what kind or where, but there they are, bursting into busy song as if they'd just arrived on a train from the south, as if the bird switch in my ears had suddenly come on.

Just as suddenly I have a goal. I get there speedily. But then a hesitation that verges on the fatal sets in. I have skied to the edge of town and can see the grocery store. I can see people steaming in and out of it. The automatic doors open to let in coated and hatted people and to let out coated and hatted people pushing silver carts with brown bags in them.

They are going to go home to warm houses, cook the food and eat it. In most cases, the probability is high that there will be other people there, possibly children and maybe animals.

I am so hungry I have a cramp in my stomach. It tilts me forward. I lean on my poles. I think I can see my checker, still greyly scanning boxes and cans and bottles, still weighing fruit and totting up the price.

I have money in my pocket. It has always been there. On the literal level, I am able to ski down the hill, unsnap the skis, walk into the grocery store and make a purchase.

But I can't. I don't have permission; I am forbidden.

I ski back into the woods, the only path open.

For a little while I ski aimlessly. George has gone off. He vanished before I watched the grocery store. I slalom through the trees, a pretty tricky maneuver on cross-country skis. The air thickens with snow-dark.

I come out at the small hill above the cabin of the stockbroker. I watch it and, though I can't see him, I do see that sure-fire sign of human habitation, smoke. I am surprised by the tide of cheerfulness this carries up to me. The snow begins again.

By the time I get back to my cabin, the snow is dense and I am high, soaring on the empty euphoria of hunger and exercise in the sterile air. I stop by the tree to finger my carving of the day before. Then I ski up to the house, swinging my butt from side to side, that hard energy in the gluteus maximus elongating in my body and out of it, up into the padded sky, down into the ligneous earth. The track I leave behind dances.

I almost don't see the carton of milk. I am looking behind me to begin with and, also, the carton is nearly covered with the new snow. I pick it up gingerly, with the farthest joints of my gloves, arms outstretched as if the cardboard were radioactive.

I can tell by squeezing that it has been left recently enough that it isn't frozen but not so recently that the tracks of whoever brought it haven't been covered.

With the carton tucked under my arms—my possession now, one to be guarded—I ski around the house. There are no tracks other than my own leading in any direction.

I take off my skis and go inside, carton still under my arm. I put it on the desk. I walk away, put some kindling in the stove, take off my coat and gloves. I sit on the couch and watch out the window. But there it is. Red with white lettering. Insistent in my peripheral vision. Not a part of the dark gray, the burgundy, the bear brown of the room, not familiar in this landscape.

I give in to its gravity. I move to the desk chair. I look at the waxed surface, the bright colors underneath, the letters. "Fields' Dairy. Homogenized Vit D," it says. This is the only clue it offers up and it is without content. I make a swipe at the carton, angry and greedy both. It catches in my claw. I set it in my lap, the opening facing me, and press the lips back. I try forcing the slit open, but I am too weak. I hold onto the carton with my knees, get my knife out of my hip pocket, and cut it.

I take a sip directly from the carton and put it back on the desk.

The taste is not altogether pleasant. I try to remember whether or not I ever liked milk. I experiment with trying to remember other tastes of fresh food—oranges or lettuce or birthday cake—and fail. I run my tongue along my upper lip. Now it tastes better, buttery and thick. I walk around the room—sauntering a little, acting nonchalant—but rush back to the desk and drink great gulps of milk.

I stop myself just before I've drunk the whole half-gallon and go outside to pour some in George's bowl. He is there, waiting. He puts his big lion's head into the bowl and virtually sucks up the white liquid.

For one single second I think I see a little black puppy head pushing its way into the bowl next to George's gold one. It's convincing enough to give me the impulse to shove her away before he attacks her, protecting his food supply from ravenous puppy appetite: there's nothing very civilized about either one of us anymore.

But a gust of gray wind blows stinging wet snow into my face and of course there's no black puppy there. Where would she have come from?

I retreat inside and George follows me. We sleep the rest of the day and all of the night.

For the next week or ten days food appears irregularly. It is always something unexpected, sometimes an incongruous combination. One day there is a red plastic net of grapefruit leaning against the house with a block of Tobler chocolate planted upright in the snow in front of it as marker. The food doesn't come every day or with any pattern I can detect. I don't ski every day and when I am home I sit on the sofa, upright in the dark, with a candle next to me on the chest, watching the window vigilantly, waiting for the coming or going of the man.

I have been awake for periods of time that are fairly recognizably days and I have slept for what may be long nights but are pretty clearly just one night at a time, not two or several with days sandwiched. I have eaten the food that is delivered to me and I have chopped. I have wondered how my advanced students are faring at Stony Brook not too seriously but enough to be noticeable.

I have thought about lovely Maria and how she is probably just as nuts as I, perhaps more so given the rigidity of her defining context. I have missed Galen badly. I have thought about my father and about Donovan. I have known that both the love I feel for them and the abyss between me and them are equally true, equally real, inevitable, undeniable, endlessly contradicting one another, never coming to rest. My mother might as well be buried in my guts and her tombstone stuck in my heart.

Mostly, I watch for the man.

I know it is a man who brings the food. Only a man would be able to figure out my erratic schedule so precisely that he knows better than I when I will be awake, when asleep, when gone. Only a man would take this sort of impersonal interest in the steady deterioration of another human being, would be willing to intervene but not take over.

Or maybe his interest isn't entirely impersonal. Maybe we have something in common. Maybe he is living in the dark too. Maybe I do not look so wild or haggard as I imagine I do. Maybe he admires the well-wornness of my fashions.

Maybe there is a luminosity that comes of having concentrated myself this way, of having withdrawn and let go of everything that wasn't required and even some of that, of having pursued the life of a snow-cloistered nun. Maybe he is attracted to me.

Maybe one day I will be watching out the window. I
will see a man in a red plaid hunting jacket and khaki pants
and big boots come out of the woods with a sack of plums
in his hand.

He will hold out his other, ungloved hand to George who
will be circling the perimeter of the clearing protectively.
George will put his head and tail down and growl. The man
won't move. He won't speak either.

I'll watch from inside. I won't call George off. That is the
man's lookout.

George creeps up to the man, head down, growl still
rumbling. I get up and go over to stand closer to the window,
off to the side. The man still doesn't look at George either,
not in the eye. George finally gets close enough to sniff the
hand. He sniffs. The man doesn't move.

George walks back to the house, then back to the man.
After one more round trip on George's part, the man rubs
George's head. He takes a Milk Bone out of his pocket that
George snatches as soon as he recognizes it. He runs a little
way off as if the man might change his mind, find the Milk
Bone irresistibly attractive for himself and take it back.
George isn't taking any chances.

The man—that is, my imagining of him—fades back
into the forest. But he comes back the next day and the next.
By the third day, George no longer challenges him. We both
have become accustomed to his apparition; already we
would miss him if he didn't come.

I, of course, never see the real man. He does leave a jar
of peanut butter, a bag of Chips Ahoy, and another carton of
milk sometime when I'm not looking. I eat the three together
and find they make an exceptional combination, a gourmet
snack. I compliment the man unreservedly albeit spiritually
on his taste.

In the daily round of activities I begin to reserve a
space for the man, to make him a domestic habit. One day,
chopping, I wonder what would happen if he really did

come out of the woods and pet George. Would he come to the house? What would happen next?

I am indoors, in the nest on the sofa. He stands outside the door not knocking. He knows full well that I am inside watching. If he took one giant step to his right he could look through the window at me. He won't, but I pull the Indian blanket over my head anyway. I feel more than a little ridiculous like that, so I push the blanket back from my head but don't otherwise take action.

The man goes away. He isn't disappointed or reproachful. He was simply advertising his intentions, a soft sell.

For one day, I hang the blanket back over the window again, but this is a more absurd action than hanging it over my head. Time will pass; the late winter day will push in, if too gently to be called rape then at least as inexorably.

The man will come back. I might as well try to get ready. I take a look around the room. It is dark even with the window bared. It is littered with clothes, cans and food wrappers, pans George has cleaned, dust balls, and dog hair.

And of course the boats.

Sooted webs festoon the corners of the room and crochet together the exposed beams in the ceiling. The door to the bedroom has not been opened in what can justifiably be called plural weeks. As far as I know, that door and the one to the kitchen now open straight outside.

The nest on the bed is amazing—deplorable by even the worst housekeeper's standards. The mass has reconstituted itself so that now what shows are red and black blankets, brown dog rug, a kelly green glove hanging helplessly over the edge, a down vest, two shoes, unmatched. The summer clothes and the boots have vanished, their season past.

And under all that—still, miraculously—the corpse of my husband, drunk, passed out, now passed on.

Well, Donovan, my one love, I have lain on you for an entire winter now. It is time for you to go.

I shake out the bedclothes—an instance of the meaning finally catching up with the word—and fold everything neatly in a pile at one end of the sofa. It still looks like weird laundry but folded now. I line up the footgear near the stove.

I take a survey of the room. It looks odd, dirty for a woman, but the only truly bizarre aspects remaining, in my opinion, are the pieces of paper on the floor.

Too bad, I say, on principle. He will just have to steer clear of the boats.

But I broom them into a corner with one foot anyway.

I look over the mess on my desk, the Hormel cans, the pile of unsorted papers, ancient bills, even older letters from which I've been tearing the scraps. There are catalogs in the pile, slick flags of color advertising clothes that I cannot imagine ever wearing again—skirts, stockings, suit jackets: silk—or even ever having worn, and for cut-rate vitamins my ethereality will only need if it chooses to body forth more radically than it now does. I push around in these long enough to get down to the paper I was working on, the tenure problem.

I sit down, stunned by the insurmountable philosophical obstacles the problem raises now in my mind. I cannot understand how I ignored them before: Alps that, arriving in Switzerland at night, one never suspected.

The very existence of the embryonic paper implies that mathematics are worthwhile, a worthy pursuit, that abstractions are valuable.

Are they?

And, avoiding that fundamental issue—setting it off in brackets for later, difficult (possible?) proof—only clears the field for the conundrum of anyone—myself in the specific case—pursuing a goal. I'm talking about any goal, any pursuit, any one. What is finally more important—the dying I am trying to do this winter or this mathematics problem? As with Mandelbrot's coastline, the answer is finite to the man with the yardstick, infinity to the snail; answerable and not; an orange felt by the right hand and the same orange held in the left.

I bracket that one too, quickly, sincerely unable to approach it and feeling the harbingers of panic as I try.

But even that idea—seeing mathematics or even death as a goal—turns out, on further reflection to be much less laughable than the concept of tenure and its place in the universe, so I pitch the latter without even bracketing it— not even a parenthesis for the tenure problem.

I leave the problem out on the desk. I leave it there with insouciance that I realize arises from my suspicion the man may know what to do with it.

The problem. The man. These are good for a laugh and I have one. But, humor notwithstanding, I am clearly waiting for him now.

He comes to the door at twilight and knocks. I have eaten and drunk nothing since knowing that he would come: the nun or the bride for the veil; the girl for the one desired date. Luckily, no food has appeared since the Chips Ahoy. I'm not at all sure how loudly my vocation could sound out against that siren song.

I am stripped, then, as thin as I can be alive, though I am still dressed in my rustic raiment—the jeans, flannel shirt, father-sweater, rag socks, intricate layers of long underwear. But I don't have the coat or shoes on anymore.

I rise from the sofa at his second set of knocks. I open the door and step back from the cold and move my gray socks away from the soon-to-be melted snow on his black cowboy boots. If he has on a hat, he takes it off now.

I had not planned to see this face. I had expected middle-aged, square, blonde-gone-to-gray solidity. A possible stockbroker. A probable divorcé. I expected gray eyes.

But this man is young, younger than I am. He's very tall, has a moustache, is very gaunt. He has coarse, thick black hair and concentrated black eyes. He looks like a cross between a gunslinger and someone from the Old Testament. He looks down at the floor and searches it with what is clearly a habit. It is impossible to tell whether the gesture denotes shyness or deceit.

He doesn't say anything. Not looking, he hands me a Christmas box of Johnnie Walker. There is something used about it, second-hand, and not only because Christmas is two months gone. The box was previously bought for someone and not given or, given, not drunk.

He sits in the armchair. I sit on the couch, arm propped on the folded clothes and legs tucked under myself primly, especially in light of how bestially I am usually curled into this same piece of furniture. The lamp on the end table next to me is on and I am watching the two of us in the sliding glass.

I, blonde and pale and thin, frosted, inclining in an inexact, humane angle against the peach of the sofa cover toward the dark, muscular man, black in the white chair, as upright as a stick of dynamite. Neither of us has said a word, the silence an unexploited coal mine, dark and dangerous, given to fire and suffocation, yet profitable, desirable, necessary: resisting the descent unimaginable.

I have put the box of liquor on the corner of the chest that inserts itself between us. I realize, the revelation of a brilliant opening chess move, that I want a drink. The epiphany, though, ends in gracelessness as I bolt forward but am suddenly arrested: there is the problem of a glass. I subside clumsily.

What kind of Virginian have I turned into? I know I am supposed to do something with the bottle—not just take but offer; also glasses are to be provided, and, of course, a small collation.

Maybe I could open a can of string beans, set it on the chest, demonstrate technique by fishing one delicate green cylinder out myself, displaying it, popping it into my mouth.

At least glasses. Glasses, for Christ's sake.

Desperation squeezed in hands praying between knees. I cannot go into the kitchen. The Thanksgiving clutter has sprung back onto the counters; I know it has. I cannot open the door.

The man intercedes. He takes the box from the chest, opens it, breaks the seal, takes a slug, puts it back on the table.

Like a Virginian moved to Texas, a civilized person experienced in the exigencies of the frontier, he takes my eyes and nods to the open bottle. I slug from it just like he did.

"I'd like to announce my intention to court you," he says. I still have the bottle in my hand. He has a troubadour's voice.

I nod, take another drink and pass it back to him. Done, offered and accepted: this promise, this threat.

He sits in the armchair every time he comes. I sit on the sofa every time. I have begun to comb my hair. I made a foray into the kitchen one night in the dark before he came. He brings the alcohol and the ice. Now there are always glasses of something condensing white rings into the surface of the chest.

He is sententious, as you might expect a gunslinger to be. He talks about an alcoholic father and a weak and dependent mother, but briefly, with no self-pity. Donovan, I see, abused me not with fists but with words, demanding not physical obedience but sympathy. Which flowed from me as blood from a broken nose. The dark man does not need this, nor does he ever ask for what he does not need.

Instead, my life pours out of me. Fire fed, glasses filled by masculine hands, night after night I talk. I try to maintain the heroic code he has brought into the house but succeed only selectively. I slide, I know, into the maudlin: my father, my husband, my dog.

I succeed in some restraint when it comes to my mother. Whenever she comes up, exactly two tears slide out of my eyes, just like out of the mannequin's blue plastic ones.

For reasons I don't quite fathom—surely the code demands only a leash, not euthanasia—I never mention the baby. Whenever that topic threatens to come to life, I turn the conversation to my work.

Which the gunslinger admires. His profession is a little vague, as is his place of residence. I, gathering signs, conjecture that he lives nearby in the forest—at least he does for this winter—and that he is some sort of professional hunter. Of things that need to be hunted, I imagine: black bears, wolves, overpopulations of deer. And he goes wherever and whenever he is called: authorities in Florida might call him to reduce a late summer crocodile census, or Wyoming might need him for a civilization-crazed rampant grizzly. He has the ambivalent professional value of a bounty hunter—a shade of depredation, a shade of heroism.

I don't quite understand his appreciation of algebra, a discipline as far removed as anything can be from tracks in the forest: one leading to warm, stinking animal flesh, the other into the farther and farther reaches of beautiful, frigid air. But, far from announcing how bad he was at it in high school (do bounty hunters take regular classes in high school? or do they follow the distributive ed. curriculum? did spurs and chains and studs rattle and jingle and gleam as he crossed the stage for his diploma?), he asks me about the problem I'm working on, and, when I trace out a part of it in the water rings on the table, he can finger in the relevant mappings. Or at least his guess is as good as mine.

Donovan lost all interest in mathematics as other matters such as himself and my betrayal of same and the durability of the liquor supply took precedence. I had forgotten the pleasures of collaboration. As traps go, it is foolproof in its mercy.

W hen an animal goes to ground," the dark one says to me one night, "sometimes the only way to get it out is to smoke it."

I nod appreciatively, then we are silent. I have remembered how to converse, though I don't remember having conversations before that are so filled with natural silences, lapses that, far from causing discomfort, are necessary to the texture of the social landscape.

"Is that rain?" I say.

We listen and then he takes my hand, leads me by instinct through the kitchen to the dining room door where he cracks the door and we listen to the sound of rain on the tin roof of the dining room. It is a palpable sound, sensual, unlike the implicative sound of snow.

The dark man leads me back to the living room where we put on coats and I boots. We go out the front door.

He has been visiting me for perhaps a month now. It was a cold, fast Marchish rain that is ending even as we come out. We walk away from the cast-out light from the lamp inside and around the side of the cabin where the light is curtained off from us and we must sense the parameters of the deck. We stomp across the erstwhile garden and go to lean against the split-rail fence around my property. We watch the maverick cloud that dropped the rain pass out of our sky.

"See that?" he says. He points upward, his dark hand and black coat discernible in the moonless night by virtue of their more dense presence, more felt than seen.

I don't see a thing.

"That silver curve?" he says.

And then, of course, I do see it. A scimitar slice, conjured as if his finger commanded a thin silver line be cut across the dome of the heavens.

"That's the power curve," he says. "Everything in front is being pushed along by it; everything in front is flying."

Roller skates, kites, gliders. I can feel their energy, the partnership with wind.

He moves his finger a little to the left. The stars in this part of the sky are much more sparse, lacking even the symmetry of fractals.

"Everything behind the power curve is being dragged," he explains.

I believe this: Orion and his fellow winter-powerful constellations are clearly in front, bunched, partly driven by the sliver of power, partly simply bullies themselves. The single stars behind the curve bedraggle.

"You're behind the power curve now," the dark one says.

I am crushed, drained, dropping as in a flying dream when shot from the sky by the improbability of it. A dark arm goes around my shoulders, propping me up against the very real possibility that I am going to fall into the iced-over snow.

"But you're just gathering strength there. Soon you'll be out in front," he says gruffly into my ear, Poppa Bear.

I straighten myself up inside my coat and the semi-circle of his arm, stamp my boots in the snow. I can feel the power already collecting in my spine; my solar plexus begins to pulse with the promised energy of the absent sun.

The man drops the dark pointing hand to my coat, which he unbuttons. He opens my shirt too and miraculously frees my breast of the layers of clothes. Exposed to the air, the nipple freezes hard. He leans over me and put his mouth on it, the dark curve of his head and back forming a black penumbra above a small silver moon.

The fires of hell surround my bedroom. I have opened the door into it and, in fact, never leave. Never leave the bed. There is a fireplace at the back of the cave I never noticed before. It stays constantly burning, though I never see the man leave the room either.

In the middle of the room is the bed in the middle of which is me in the middle of which is the gun metal of the man's cock, pushing coldly, completely inside me, splitting my hot body in two with icy steel. The room is suffocating.

He talks all the time. He talks about devices and chains and foreign objects. He tells stories about other women who might be there too or women he wishes were there instead. Sometimes other men are involved in the narrative, sometimes with me. He tells about doing what we are doing on empty highways in the desert and in public places, against the hood of a car while people in a crowd watch.

When the dark one slaps my ass and calls me a cunt, I am both abject and alive. When I can think, I wonder at the quality of mercy. In this case, there is a slime of sophistication about it. I think of an inarticulate black bear and how this thin hard cold alloy bisects me where the other enveloped and yet in both cases it is my mind, my heart, my delicious corpse.

The fucking goes on far too long. He never comes and is proud of it. It goes on for days. I sleep and wake and he is still pushing, still cursing. His cock is immense, diabolic, the instrument not of fallen man. I accept him in every conceivable way and almost never resist or gag.

As desperate, as pulverized, as far gone as I am, at even crazier times I am also watching. It is as if the affair was taking place at a department meeting and my body has been tabled. Its reactions—its strong animal urges, its seductiveness and power as well as its perversities and degradations—the way my ass hits the table in uncontrollable rhythmic spasms as I come, the indecipherable ululations from my throat—are being noted, graphed by the mathematical me.

If it is true that the me writhing, powerful and pinned, on the bed feels no shame, then it is also certainly true that the me who observes passes no judgment. We simply wonder how far I'll go.

But when it seems all the possibilities are necessarily exhausted, when my flesh seems atomized over who knows how long a time, the dark one has one more trick up his sleeve, one more lesson to teach. I wake up and he is gone. Although the fire is still lit, there is not even his scent on the sheets. He never comes back. He goes as silently and absolutely back into the night as he had come from it. He leaves me to barbecue in the inferno.

I don't leave the bedroom. The fire dies down and I sit all that night waiting. I sit naked on the edge of the bed, my hands clasped together between my knees.

And then another night I wait outside, standing at the curve in the road around which I have certain knowledge he eventually will have to come.

For reasons not entirely rational—what has rationality to do with this situation?—I am sure that he routinely drives down this road. He lives on this road, as a matter of this kind of fact, just slightly beyond where I do.

I stand a little off the road passing near my cabin on the side of the house opposite to the garden. Dressed in a black pea coat, black jeans, black boots and no gloves or hat, I shelter among the trees lining the top of the small rise between the road and the property.

I have a dark-barreled shotgun held carelessly along my right leg, the index finger of my right hand not through the hook but lodged negligently in the trigger housing. For the moment I am not watching myself. I am all there.

In the dark distance, I hear the engine of an old pickup truck power down to make the turn from the highway onto this—my—road. I check with my left hand to be sure the barrel is smoothly in place, loaded.

The highway is pretty far away so I still wait, carelessly.

The truck takes the curves and I follow it through each one. Then the muscles in my back and down my right arm collect themselves imperceptibly as I hear the pickup downshift again to start up the twisted grade that plateaus and straightens just before it reaches me.

He is passing the place where the fairy girl vanished. The truck shifts up prematurely. It has lost power as its lights crest the hill.

As he comes over the top, the dark one sees a person in black but with extremely pale face and hair and hands step out of the trees. He is alarmed at first that he will hit her.

But that turns out not to be what he should fear.

She is facing the direction from which he is coming. As his truck hurtles toward her bend, her left side swings parabolically so that her left foot points to the road where the truck will soon be and her left arm describes the same truncated curve of dark air and meets the gun barrel at her crotch as her right hand lifts it.

Together the hands lift the dark gun up, a double will-o-the-wisp supporting the double barrel, luminescence and deadliness now within his headlight glare. The hands nestle the gun firmly against her shoulder. She follows the truck's inevitable trajectory.

Her finger is on the trigger; she knows where the center of the driver's side of the windshield is and she orders her body to fire as the gun points to the passenger's side, knowing the lag.

She fires.

She is knocked back; the windshield explodes; the head shatters.

Then the woods are dark again. She is standing in the trees again, waiting again.

CHAPTER EIGHT:

Beltane

It takes about fifty-five repetitions of this scene before I can drop off to sleep.

The fog begins to roll up the mountain from the lake at the bottom. Why does the supposed improvement in weather—the possibility of spring—bring something so much worse: suffocating, wet, permeating air? I watch it surround my cabin as I lie in bed with just the storm door closed or stand at the sliding deck doors in the living room.

Completely naked now, I touch my emaciated, sinking flesh experimentally. The fire in the bedroom is gone, along with the fireplace. I am still warm even in there, perhaps feverish, or burning a spirit-fire.

I regret the loss of clarity to the winter air, but even more the loss of the food, which no longer comes.

It is that, and not the dark one, which disappeared. This is a wild guess: I have been waiting for the dark man to return and then been standing on the roadside of my imagination with a shotgun for something resembling two days. I am hungry.

I have never seen the person who fed me. I don't know why he or she did it, how long I was fed, or why the person stopped.

It fed an experiment, though, an excursion into the possibility that a man might rescue me, into my own hopefulness. It was something of a surprise that the experiment lead to perversity, abandonment, and revenge. But, then, that is the nature of experiment, isn't it? One isn't supposed to know where it's going to take one.

So there you are, Ma, by definition.

Many people do not think of mathematicians as experimentalists, but this—like so many professional expectations—is inaccurate. How do you suppose we come up with some of the problems we do—like calculating the distance between skew lines—nevermind the solutions? You must guess there is some sense of fun, some childish excitement over the possibility of being surprised, even dreadfully so.

We mathematicians are looking for something new, something to take us beyond the boundaries of established theory. It seems that everything that could be cooked up, has been, but still nothing is resolved. There are structures, sets, categories, and mappings for what seems like every conceivable situation. There are theories so satisfying, you'd be sure they would put an end to the matter.

But still we are discontent, still restless. Still, somehow and somewhere, problems continue to proliferate, planes go down, lovers fight, children die; wars continue or break out all over again. There is turbulence.

So we continue to relentlessly, maniacally, pursue a result.

And—don't lose sight of this, Ma—we are secretly grateful that there are none, that we are still called upon to invent, still needed, still alive and twisting on the hook.

I watch the little stream just beyond my back fence in the afternoon. I have on my winter clothes again, though they now feel to me like a casing. Similarly, the stream is encased in ice. The formations of ice on the surface are beautiful, frozen in fluid, graceful shapes above the sliding, frigid water beneath that carries in it leaves and sticks but no life yet, no minnows or water bugs.

There are no tracks out here, no signs a dark man walked across my dead garden to lean against the split-rail fence and look at black heaven on Valentine's Day or anytime thereafter. It does not bother me.

My invention of a diabolic man does not bother me. I don't mind that I have blown him away.

I lean against the fence on the other side, looking back toward the cabin. Cold, damp, gray air comforts my face.

Who is to say, I ask you, that a woman's depravity—this tendency toward self-autopsy—is any more or less perverse than a man's tendency to drink and womanize? Are we not equal in these separate ways? Who is to say that these things don't mean being alive, to both of us?

So we women lay our lovely bodies on the steel table, make the incision from clavicle to pubis, disembowel, hand out our viscera, our hearts, our wombs and their products, our healthy vaginas, our lips and ear lobes, our pink nipples, our livers and more. We eviscerate and wait for appreciation: a round of applause, a kiss, a phonecall.

Of course, the doctors tell us, there are cures: live alone, marry a nice man.

But, you know, Ma, I still am not convinced. I'm not sure I would choose health when I can see little distinction between salvation and taxidermy. And I don't know, but I think you would agree; I suspect you made the same choice, Ma—pro-autopsy, if you could not live the dancing life.

The house, not so warm now but holding the memory of warmth, takes its foggy daughter back in.

When I sleep that night, the truck annihilation fades. I am relieved of civilization on an even deeper level than before.

A wolf, released from captivity after having been used in a wolf- or bear-baiting show or maybe only as the object of observation in a circus that was just as violent, as assaulting— is that much more committed to the woods on her return. After enslavement, her loyalty to the wild is absolute. She runs fifty miles in a day. She is stripped clean of the belief that civilization will protect and feed her.

But the wolf returned from captivity will not kick up her heels—she will not gambol or bark; she will certainly not toss a broken bough up in the air in joy.

No, it is only in the way she trots—easily, unhurriedly— through the snow toward the pines, only by a glance behind her as she hits the edge of the forest, a trotting flash of her eyes over her shoulder at the place she has escaped—only by these signs can you catch a glimpse of the contempt she has for what is gone.

The dark partner was no solution. Neither was Donovan or the house or the job.

In the morning, I am standing at the kitchen sink and that much I know. I take a sip of French Roast I have made myself. I picture Better Boy seedlings in the back kitchen window.

I am not alarmed at those subtractions, of marriage to Donovan, the Stony Brook house, the Stony Brook job. Many of them are simply the erasure of what was not there to begin with: a belief in the beneficence of institutions.

But I am alarmed—and disturbed at my alarm—over the absence of food deliveries.

The coffee detonates in my stomach and the tomato plants in my mind straggle and die. I unhook the back window and push it up and open to look outside for George with more sense of urgency than I have felt for days—weeks? or, Lord, months?

I go blank again for some time, perhaps only hours this time; the violent taste of coffee, of everything, recedes. When I come back, I am in the living room and George is on the deck, outside the glass doors, big and gold and wagging his tail. I let him in.

He still has mass, his big bone structure, but he is thinner and his coat much more ragged. His puppiness—a lifelong trait in a Golden—has turned ancient.

"Tell you the truth," I say to him, "don't know where I've been."

He sits on the floor, attending, wagging the last joint of his tail once.

"How much do you know?" I ask him. "The dark man? How long? How long shooting?"

These are stupid questions to George, but he humors me. He does not reproach me for being mentally absent all this time. But he's clearly glad to have me back. There is something nervous about him, something that suggests experiments are all well and good, but there comes a time when they become self-consuming; there is a vanishing point.

Something about George's nervousness is a warning to me.

"The Milk Bones were real?" I ask him. "Nutritionally complete? You crave them over hot rabbit?"

The great forehead wrinkles up like a Shar-pei's. I find the strain unbearable: the impossible directive to put the air mask on one's own face before you give air to the fainting child. The compression in my house has suddenly, sickeningly, dropped.

Or maybe it has been dropping gradually these last two days.

Because it has been two days exactly since the food stopped. I can calculate this accurately all of a sudden, based on I'm not sure what.

But I know this as clearly as if I've heard an alarm. I wake up into time as if my mind had been registering its passing with the accuracy of an atomic clock, up to the nanosecond, whether or not anyone was looking.

Going back to sleep is no longer an option. I decide to go outside, aware that something out there has set off an alarm. George agrees completely; he paws the door, crosses the room, paws my knee, back to the door but this time with anxiety crackling his fur.

I don't have any clothes on, it turns out. I look around the living room for the clothes I had on the day before, but there is not a stitch to be found there. The laundry pile has disappeared.

It has exploded all around the bedroom. So I have in fact been living in here during this period of thrall to the flesh. I untangle my long underwear from the blankets. I have trouble finding one ski shoe that I eventually locate just outside the bedroom door. The result of a mad moment, I imagine, of tipping it up for the champagne in it and then a gay toss out the door.

I am sturdily if awkwardly dressed. I seem to have lost the self-dressing faculty or had it impaired somewhere along the line. Off I go. George gallops out the door and into the woods while I put on skis and then I join him.

My best guess is that it is mid-April now. There is still a long time left to last frost, even till last snow. Onions can't be planted yet; pansies would be ravaged and die. Today the sky and the land are both still covered with snow; the mountains in the distance rise above the timberline and straight into the clouds with no distinction in color, the whole scene wrapped in chilly unspun lamb's wool.

But there is something about the light—nothing promising but rather a diffusion of its crystal sharpness— that suggests the coming excesses of spring. Occasionally I can hear a bird sing out, abruptly bursting forth and then an immediate arrest, as if he'd made a mistake, spoken too soon.

I am weak, I find, a little slushy from the excesses of imagination. But there is an element of strength, a substance in my legs and up my back that is new since the last, emptily euphoric ski. The thin axe blade of my body has been tempered.

I am grateful to the food deliverer for this strength. I know that without him I would not have it, might not have a body at all.

I am grateful even though the deliveries and their abjuration have broken me, have been a trail of breadcrumbs leading back to the territory of the living and desire and its attendant anxiety.

I can tell I'm looking for him because my stride is no longer free; it is curtailed by wanting. My pace is anxious, staccato. I go up blind alleys into trees so dense I have to turn around to get out. I try again.

I would like to stop trying, to go home or at least to stop caring. But none of these has probability. There is no more rest for me; the season for legitimate hibernation is over.

I know I have found what I'm looking for as soon as I see the cabin George and I stopped by earlier in the winter, the one with the man covering the woodpile. The house is still there; so are the woodpile and the tarp. But the smoke isn't.

His house is closer to mine than I realized the first time, no more than half a mile down the road past my cabin. The wood is blonder, the windows in general larger, more daring. It sits in the middle of a stand of silver birches.

There is something green in one of the smaller windows, a kind of natural flag, or wink. I ski closer. He could be simply gone, but the plant in the window says this isn't so.

I want to freeze. All instincts tell me this would be the wise choice: don't go any farther; call someone.

I know I am about to know something that I might not be able to bear knowing.

But stasis will not save me; it will not stop me from intersecting with consciousness. Avoidance is an empty term; knowledge is a professional hunter.

The cabin is still.

The ivy-leafed geranium lures me on.

I stand outside its window, hands on the sill, skis to one side, and look inside past the now-curling leaves of the still pinkly, gaudily flowering plant.

Petals are on the inside sill. The man lies just beyond them. He has on the hunting jacket, jeans and boots. His face still looks grayly kind, middle-aged, stock-brokerish. But it is still and ash gray. This man is a dead; this is a fact, just like my mother is dead.

I don't want to, but I go to the door, snap off my skis and turn the handle. The door is unlocked. I walk in, go to him, kneel beside him and touch his face. It is not entirely cold. I look around, see a plastic bag nearby, past his body a woodstove still emanates warmth. He has not lain here long—a day, not a week. He is not dead.

I scramble up from my knees, look frantically for a telephone, find one on the desk and call the rescue squad.

When the paramedics have come, strapped oxygen onto the man who moaned as they moved him onto the stretcher, and taken him away, blaring, I am left alone in the woods outside his cabin again.

I begin to back up, but the felt strips on the bottom of my skis stick and the skis torque and twist from under my feet. I hear a branch breaking under the weight of wet snow, the beginning of what will clearly be an endless series of sonic booms thundering through my head.

As the branch falls from high above me, crashing through living limbs, it occupies my brain, releases me from the frozen state, and I succeed in turning around. I ski with fast, short economical strides, arms bunched around poles held in fists—a kind of running—straight back to my cabin.

I fall instantly and mercifully into a soggy gray sleep. The boom becomes a kind of music, something for my brain to keep itself occupied with so that it doesn't think or, God forbid, remember.

I am ripped out of sleep, finally, by the sound of someone calling my name.

She can be heard clearly, piercingly, through the booms and sleep. Her voice can be heard so well because she is my mother.

The real you, Ma. I recognize your voice as if I'd just talked to you on the phone.

You're calling my name with a clarity that, without alarm or importunity, is absolutely compelling. You are a statement of fact; you call my name as a person might initiate counting: "one."

"Amelia."

More will follow.

I cannot disobey your command. But when I am fully awake I am catapulted directly into anguish over being compelled by you, but I don't know to what.

I begin to prowl the cabin, back and forth in the living room, stoking the fire with almost every pass, then I branch out into the bedroom, then the kitchen. Finally, when nothing more will fit in the stove, I open the dining room doors into both the bedroom and kitchen. Finally, I can make the circuit again. As I walk, you talk to me. "Talk" is not the right word. You urge. You urge one thing. That I go to the hospital, see the man.

There is something in your urging that has the flavor of the obligation some cultures —Native American, legendary?— teach that one takes on when one has saved someone else's life. But what do you know of Native American culture? I don't think Birmingham belles can be Native American. Nevertheless, I am compelled by your reasoning. I eat a can of sweet potatoes, at your behest. I manage somehow to find what I'm thinking might be appropriate hospital-visiting clothes, put on coat and gloves and ski shoes. I go outside and look at the Saab, humped with snow. It is not possible that it was ever anything other than a natural part of this landscape. I put on the skis and ski toward town and the hospital.

Inside, your voice leaves me, but people do not look at me as if I am the alien I feel myself to be. I explain that I want to visit my neighbor, that I found him and called the rescue squad. Staff members seem also to assume that this makes me somehow responsible—are they Native Americans too? I find his room, go in. He is looking out the window, away from me, but knows I am there, who I am. I take his hand.

Over the next few days, he spins his story.

He was a stockbroker, after all, divorced but not recently. His wife, taking a look around her in the 1970's, wanted someone both more ambitious than he, with more backbone, and someone also exquisitely sensitive to her needs. Her next husband, she told herself, was more adequate.

The man accepted the divorce though he had never wanted one himself. He was a kind man, really, doing the best he could. He did not want the executive life, did not care whether or not he climbed the career ladder. He would have responded to his wife's needs if he could have understood what she wanted.

For himself, alone, he preferred the garden over either office or living room. He preferred weeding to power lunching; a bed of carnations on Long Island, now that was ambition. He looked at me and smiled for this first time when he told me this, albeit ruefully.

His wife kept the children away from him when they were little so he could concentrate on his work and, later, she took custody of them with ferocity, as if she were afraid he would infect them with something, possibly calm. What he would have liked, if it could have been had, was to have his small, bowl-haircutted son in the garden next to him, sitting or working, either one, with the serenity of a prince's son.

But that life was over, and so was the one after the divorce, living alone in the apartment in the city. He had taken early retirement and come to these mountains, surpassing the Catskills where many of his coworkers had houses. Those intermediate mountains seemed to him a compromise. This once he was going to follow his own tide all the way out.

He had monthly checks sent to his wife automatically and settled into his quiet life in the mountains.

He had been here several years and loved it, or perhaps love was too rambunctious a word. The only problem he'd found was with the shortness of the growing season, only from Memorial Day to Labor Day, but he had found ways to have green around anyway: the windows.

It had all been enough until this winter, which had begun to wear on him. There was wood chopping, of course, and skiing. Other than that, there was just subsidence. This year it had begun to feel like erosion.

When he got to the part where he began to notice me, he talked about me distantly, as if I weren't both listener and subject. His telling was rueful, and had a sort of self-irony about it that made it me think that that quality came along with living in these woods in the winter.

He'd seen me before, he supposed—more revealed in cottons at the grocery store over the summer—but I had been indistinguishable from the mass of summer people. I hadn't really made an impression on him until the fall began, maybe not until around Halloween, when my Saab became virtually the only vehicle besides his that came down this road.

"You were a pretty good distraction for a while," he said. "I knew you weren't a girl really. I suppose my wife would scold me for calling you that. I knew you were really a woman—not pretty exactly but interesting looking. Lanky and blonde, a body that did what it was told, a deep grove between your eyes that indicated a capacity for concentration and puzzlement, the alert watchfulness of a not perfectly defended animal; your dogs." He checked to see if I was offended by the "not pretty exactly" remark. I reassured him that he was talking to a mathematician. What had "pretty" to do with it?

By the third of my visits to the hospital, we began to walk the halls together. He had introduced himself as

Malcolm Keller by that time and reported that the doctors were keeping him for observation.

"The first time I noticed you I was walking in the forest and saw you outside your house. You were wrapped in some black fabric like a cloak and talking to your dogs. I got close enough to see that it was a blanket you had on, but I didn't know why. Your inexplicable behavior clearly had its own justification that I couldn't fathom but could admire. You were the last one left living on the road after all the summer and fall people had gone. After the blanket day, I began to walk near your house frequently and to look when I drove by or to watch for you on the road."

He noticed details: the two dogs often seen in the back seat of the car, a black head slightly lower and more delicate than the gold one, both alert with ears forward and giving the quality of attention to the passing scenery that showed how pleased they are to be going somewhere with me.

"I saw you outside often, though you never seemed to notice me," he said. We were sitting in the solarium, warm and yellow inside. "You were busy with chores, chopping wood or shoveling snow. In dark winter clothes and with fair hair uncovered, you moved quickly and assuredly around your house, chopping, slogging through the snow, balling it up to splatter on one of the dogs for whom this was almost impossibly fun and to whom you talked continuously. You were completely unembarrassed about this form of talking to yourself and were loud about it," he said with a rare chuckle.

He didn't have to get very close to hear me admonish the dogs to remember things I didn't want forgotten, like tomato paste to be added to the grocery list, or to ask them where a lost glove was, or the adze. Sometimes he heard me inquire of the dogs what they thought someone named Donovan would think of a particular situation. I had, he said, the self-sufficiency of a child at play.

Malcolm had the idea at Thanksgiving that he would visit me. He had already called his own children in the morning and received their lukewarm holiday wishes. Something about me struck him as more like him than his own children—perhaps the self-sufficiency, but maybe it was just the lack of accusation, he said. But by the time he drove down to my house, another car was already there.

Outside of a slight regret not to have my company, he was delighted for me. He was not a man to define himself by possession. The house looked even from the outside more warm and alive than it ever had before, red and yellow bubbling inside a circle of intimacy circumscribed by snow. He drove on.

After that I was alone again, he saw.

"I resolved to invite you over for Christmas," he said. "But just before that I saw you in the woods near my house with the one gold dog. Come to think of it, I hadn't seen the border collie for some time. And you—whom I thought of as the girl-woman by then—had lost some of your imperviousness. From inside my house I saw you in the woods. You looked like a hunted animal. I put on my jacket and gloves and went outside to cover the woodpile to give you an excuse to talk to me if you wanted."

He paused for a moment and looked at me. By now I was the one having trouble holding a gaze. I crimped the denim of my jeans while he smoothed the blanket I'd put over his knees.

"But you vanished while my back was to you," he said. "I decided to leave you alone. You seemed to crave solitude."

And then at Christmas his usual peaceful mood had deepened and grown more gray. He wasn't exactly unhappy. It seemed like a more complex layer of acceptance. He lay down in his melancholy as if on a bed of gray satin-covered feathers. He sank farther and farther into it as the winter progressed.

Starting in mid-February he roused himself by taking special treats to the girl-woman.

"I enjoyed trying to think of the very things your body would feel delight over, whether or not your spirit was any longer able to respond. I could imagine these things fairly well, I thought, because the two of us were on parallel tracks, travelling in isolation," he said.

I had begun to hear a poetry in his telling—if not Yeats then at least something equal to what Donovan could conjure.

But finally Malcolm's mood grew more compellingly sorrowful and, anyway, spring was coming: the girl-woman would be all right.

He let go and slid down into the darkness that had been waiting for him so long. He had read up on the Hemlock Society's method of self-annihilation and had dutifully taken the large dose of over the counter sleeping pills and vodka.

"I got so drunk, though," he told me with a rueful laugh, "I passed out before I put the plastic bag over my head."

I held his hand and we watched an avalanche of wet snow slide off an evergreen outside the solarium glass.

A week after I found Malcolm, I lose him again. When I go to the hospital, he isn't in his room. I buttonhole a doctor I've seen talking to him before.

"Mr. Keller was not willing to agree not to try to attempt suicide again," he says when he finds out I'm the only person who has visited Malcolm. "He was committed to the mental hospital for further treatment."

I don't ask where the mental hospital is—I'm pretty sure it's not skiing distance and I'm not up to unburdening my car.

I dive into the oubliette of sleep again, but only briefly.

When I wake up, I know this much: Malcolm had been living in a more recognizable despair than mine, had tried to help me but was overwhelmed by the need to obliterate himself. No connection to me could have made this different. Although he offered the only help I had that winter, I was not enough to keep him from his need to find comfort in the arms of mortality.

So the snow has taught me this lesson. I have accepted its tutelage.

And the snow brings with it another avalanche: although my father had offered me tids and bits of love, he had always been dead to me. His diabolism existed only insofar as I needed it to, only insofar as I needed to twist my own power into something more sensational than what my father actually registered. A kind man, doing the best he was able, whose only violence against me was to withdraw from life and not allow me to have any real impact on him— to inadvertently cheat me of drama.

But underneath this lesson, given and accepted, is something vastly more perilous—a ship already sunk, a plane taking off with one, faulted engine.

Because it isn't the metaphorical death of my father or Malcolm's near death that is eating me alive. These deaths I can understand. The failing of men—the offer of assistance which cannot be followed through—is simply an imperfection, a little weakness I forgive all too easily.

And who is it who taught me this tolerance, this global acceptance of masculine foibles? Who but my mother—you, Ma?

Taught me to give and to sympathize. But whose disappearance left me bereft, empty-handed, with nothing more to give. Whose aborted collusion left me with no one to sympathize with me.

Whose leaving taught me to handle my own pain with chores and self-effacement.

Left me with only one thing: enough time to repudiate you, at least to repudiate your orientation to home and family.

Left me early enough to choose mathematical chores over domestic ones, abandoned me early enough to choose numerical division over cell division or even pea-splitting.

Suddenly I am violently discontent. Coordinates of time and self take on a manic energy that flies off the page, my body charged with arrow-pointed trajectories that say it all and say nothing.

It takes almost the whole night to conjure this possibility, but in the wee hours, I tell the desperate story of what life would have been like if you'd lived, Ma. I lie on the bed naked, delivered up, to tell it.

My childhood was spent with you in closeness. You were always there, always holding me. And, frankly, you were always also holding me back.

There were the swimming lessons I didn't take because you were afraid of them, the lack of ballet classes because you thought they would hurt my feet. You let me stay home from kindergarten and would have let first grade go by if you hadn't been more afraid of the authorities than longing to keep me home.

Still, it was a lovely girlhood. Not every girl gets her mother's full-time attention; not every mother is more a playmate than a boss. You were always somewhere in the house and could be readily lured away from your tasks to read me Hans Christian Anderson, or, later, to play Barbie. When you were baking a pie, I assisted by fashioning dough hair-dos on the head of a heavy green-glass Coke bottle. You would make a hair-do, too, on another bottle.

Mind you, there are some drawbacks to being your best friend—like having to be loyal to you, defend you when you're under attack, or think you are. Never mind you're forty and I'm eight. You resent Grandmother and her ownership of Father. You take me into the kitchen while Grandmother is at our house for lunch and complain to me about Grandmother's sitting opposite your husband, at the foot of the table, while you sit on his right, near the kitchen.

This is a problem, because I don't, on my own, have anything against Grandmother. It's true she will never qualify for that Betty Crocker Award and all the award implies about self-sacrifice. She hates a house and everything about it. She never decorated hers after Grandfather built it for her, never painted it and certainly never hung curtains. But she has the most gorgeous gardens in town. Can't there be something said about that?

She doesn't care for the grandchildren and she doesn't have anything to do with me if she can help it, but I accompany her into the garden sometimes, making a pest of myself but trying to keep that to a minimum. From the little she tells me, from the way she looks, I can see she was never a happy woman—her husband drank and her children were for the most part a burden— but she is content in the gardens, on the terraced beds of roses and lilies, snowdrops and tradescantia.

She accepts lunch invitations from Father because she has to eat and isn't about to start cooking for herself at this late date; because he is her favorite child, her masterpiece, as she is sure she told my mother (so why can't the young woman accept this and behave accordingly?); and because she believes on some level very deeply in the idea of family. It is the closest she comes to religion, outside the garden.

But it is a sacrifice, going to dine. She has to put her tools in the basket and the basket in the cellar, change into at least a clean gardening dress, scrub her hands even though the black line encrusted under her nails has been undislodgeable for years, say goodbye to the garden and go next door to her son's house.

The wife is nice enough, really, though something of a flibbertigibbet, a fussy mother to that quiet daughter, but otherwise inoffensive. The wife would never have been able to carry on a conversation about transplanting the rhodies, which must be done right after lunch, and she has the bad habit of hanging curtains at the windows.

Grandmother finds she must remove the obstruction, twist your ironed white curtains up and pin them with books on top of the bookshelves as soon as she comes in the house. She doesn't think of this as a favor, really, though it does improve the quality of everyone's life to be able to see the outdoors; she is not service-oriented. It is a necessity, without which she cannot breathe.

I have to admit that I have some sympathy for Grandmother's point of view. Perhaps claustrophobia is inherited, but from whom? Both you and she had it. But your outrage demands my collusion and any attempt to defend Grandmother—even as now, in my own mind—is a betrayal. I whisper as furiously as you in the kitchen between courses, behind the swinging door. Father the judge doesn't acknowledge the spite among his women.

When Grandmother dies and we move into her house, you have it painted champagne white and hang curtains at every one of the many windows Grandmother had designed to let in the light and let herself out. Still, you aren't always happy there; we are all a little haunted.

When I am a teenager, you and I begin fighting, I for independence, you to keep me within the boundaries of what you consider recognizable. I win the fight long enough to get out of town for college, but I come back home at the end of it, marry, and produce offspring.

You and I see each other every day. You like the idea of grandchildren, but aren't interested in taking care of them. You resent my children sometimes—when you want me to yourself, to shop or go for lunch or have another midday glass of white wine. You don't say so. You say it's for me, in my interests, a break from my domestic duties. You are still holding on to me, in the vise-like grip of the weak, which one cannot break, except by destroying them, and incurring permanent guilt.

So I go on, not exactly unhappy, feeling vaguely claustrophobic. It seems like every year I grow afraid of something else. Two years ago, I gave up driving and my husband does all of that. This year I became afraid of snow and dread the enclosure each winter gray sky threatens. I keep my children home with me as often as possible.

I realize I am being driven by someone else's weakness and you too would have escaped if you could have, but I cannot break out of the circle of your narcissistic love without—let me be frank—depriving us both of the source of life. So I watch my sexuality fade, my power; I watch myself devour my children.

By dawn I realize how grateful I am for your death. I sleep.

But not for long. I'm pretty sure it is still the same day. I wake up with an even more insane restlessness. I rush into my clothes, out the door, and into my skis.

The landscape is monochromatic; not only is all the color washed out but all sound has been hushed by the hiss of snow. It is late afternoon. I stop for a moment, with difficulty—I am that jittery—to clear out with one finger the snow that has collected in my carving. I ski off across the sea of snow.

This time I come out very quickly above the village. Instead of turning back into the forest, I go down the hill and begin to ski around the bowl holding the town, keeping my distance. It is dusk by now and lights go on in the houses.

I ski above the grocery store. Very few people are inside, none I recognize. I see the post office on the far side of town and ski cautiously toward it. No one is in the streets around it. I go up to the building, also deserted, and bend to release my skis. The part of the post office where mailboxes are is unlocked. I can remember the combination but not the number of my box. I try ones that are full of letters and ones that are empty. None I try is right.

I come outside and am caught in the crossfire of a snowball fight. The children are yelling and don't see me. I flatten against the door, palms against the glass. The children move farther down the street. I fumble with my skis, positioning the toe of one wrong and then missing the other one altogether as I snap the binding on nothing. Finally I ski up to the forest in a panicked hurry.

When I get to the woods I call for George. I recollect he was with me until I got to the town and then he disappeared. I don't remember anymore which direction my house is in, but I begin pushing through the snow toward my best guess. I can't find the right rhythm for my stride.

At some point the dark overtakes the day, but the snow also stops and the sky clears. A nearly full moon rises. I stand in thick woods. The pines are giantesses out here, in monstrously outsized ball gowns, surrounding me menacingly but unintentionally so. I turn around, moving my skis by inches so they won't cross either in front or back and trip me into the snow. Stopping the awkward revolution arbitrarily, I ski off between the trees again. Lifting a gloved hand, interrupting my stride, I wipe my cheek with the back of it. The leather pole strap scrapes my skin.

In another clearing I stop again and call for George. He doesn't come. Then, my voice rebounding from the trees and echoing up through them to the moon, I call for Galen.

My voice is round with hope. As I turn around I trip over my skis and fall. I feel the panic freezing into a mass inside my abdomen. I think how easy, how nice, how peaceful to curl into the snow nest here. The ice sends seductive crystal fingers through my jeans, begging my warm blood to join.

But some more lively part of me assigns me a problem, something basic, something that has been done: find the point the sum of whose distances from the vertexes of a given triangle is the smallest. I begin to work it, remember the theorem about equilateral triangles and the independence of the position from the sum of the distances to the point.

After a few moments I get up, jabbing my poles into the snow harder than is necessary to pull up on.

And then abruptly, improbably, I am home. I don't know it at first and try to figure out what is familiar about the particular maple I'm looking at. When I figure it out, I am more angry.

I call for George: "Come here, God damn it."

Wind sends snow across itself.

Curtly, I ski to the door. When I reach it, though, I hesitate. There is nothing there, no sustenance. The austere cabin can in no way contain what I feel. It will explode if I go inside, ignite finally from the fires I never put out in the bedroom.

I take off my gloves and skis, leaving them heaped next to the door. I use the poles to get me back to the tree. By now, I have no way to rein myself in.

I look at the tree. With some consideration—clearly false, the kind one uses when drunk—I drop one pole in the snow and lift the other.

With a two-handed swing, I hit the tree with the pole, its clang eaten up by the old wood. As the frail metal bends I call for Donovan, my voice at first ironic and then invoking.

When one pole is twisted into uselessness, I use the other.

I call for them all, a catalog of the dead and missing. Donovan. Galen. Malcolm. Father. George.

Mother Mother Mother.

Unappeased when both poles are destroyed, I hit the tree with bare hands. By the time I feel the pain I am calling my own name, with the confused and half laughing thought I am the other Amelia who, once an expert pilot, had dropped her plane into the sea.

Still, it was you and me who kept the conversation going in that house—even our fights had more authenticity, contact, blood than any other transaction there.

You are beautiful and warm, physical and imaginative. You are a generous and silly, sexy and timid woman. We stay in contact through phone calls and perfect posture. As you grow old, your hair fades, you have a pacemaker put in. The illnesses and jealousies and uncertainties of your middle years are past. You grow, in a gentle and contented way, more silly.

You cannot add either, but you have an uncanny grasp of some of the problems I'm working on. We are far apart, and we have achieved an unquiet, alive sort of peace—one based on anger, and grief, and the deceptions of love. We have been suffocated and released in the nick of time. Our love is more stable for its volatility, resting as it does on past, and humor, and knowledge.

You are a young woman misplaced in farm life but accepting your choice while your child steps off and away, carrying with her the curse and gift of imagination.

You are even younger, unmarried. In New York a professional photographer shoots your photograph in the studio. You have dark brown hair gathered in a loose chignon, a slight contrast in color to your black velvet dress. You have your head bowed beautifully over your hands. There is a gardenia pinned on your shoulder. The flower throws the same light as your skin. There is everything about the curve of your neck of grace and life and redemption.

When I wake up, deep in the pile on the couch, my knuckles are swollen and caked in blood. George, present by some miracle I don't remember, is watching me. I get up, put wood on the fire and heat a can of soup. I feed some to George and clean my hands. After I eat, I sleep through the day and night.

I'm woken up by the phone ringing. Coming out of the depths, I take a moment to remember I'd had it reconnected one day on the way to the hospital, thinking I might want to check on Malcolm by phone sometime. It is Roger calling.

"Amelia," he says, no reproach in his tone, perhaps a little sympathy. "The divorce is final."

"Okay," I say. I can't get my mind around this idea. Did Donovan go to court? Did anyone? Was there something to sign and did I do it? I vaguely remember giving Roger a complete power of attorney. I'm standing next to the telephone table and check the window for any signs of disbelief. There are none.

"I wanted to let you know, too, that I ran across something I think you might be interested in," Roger goes on. Not even he is interested in the details of my divorce. His voice is tentative now, questioning, that of my old friend.

"Yes?" I say.

"When I went by your house after the closing, there was this dog in the yard—no collar or tags. It's more of a puppy, tan and black, maybe a shepherd of some sort. I put signs up and called the SPCA, but no one has claimed her. I wanted to know if you'd like me to bring her up there."

The last part he says in a great rush and I'm pushed backwards by it, end up sitting on my peach-colored sofa.

"I don't know, Roger, I don't know."

"I understand," he says.

I hang up and give in.

Today I have gotten up with the sun, eaten, dressed my hands, and watched George through the window as he patrols the perimeter of our territory.

I have found a pack of notebook paper buried on the desk. By the afternoon, the sun is strong enough that it warms me through the window. I pull the armchair to the window and sit with paper on book on knee. I have taken off the sweaters.

I can feel the raw skin under the bandages. I feel my whole body raw, flayed cryosurgically. I will not risk contact with any more people yet. I don't mean to starve, though, and I believe that I will grow new skin.

A smell burns up my nose, rising from my body, from between my breasts. For a moment I believe that it is the smell of sex, of Donovan, the smell that is almost stink but is desire.

But then I know, with no need for conscious memory, that it is really the stink of birth—under all these skins, this child.

I thought it was Donovan I wanted.

But it's not Donovan, not Daddy.

I know now, like knowing the value of n, it's you I wanted, Ma. You.

And now, here, alone in the great white silence of your absence, I am opening the door to life, the same way I opened it to you.

The wolf turns and turns in the warm blackness of her cave. She goes to the opening and cuffs one of her cubs who is playing with the other just outside the cave opening. She patrols the area around her cave, flushes a pheasant into hysterical flight.

The wolf's body goes rigid, automatically freezing into hunting posture. But she relaxes.

She has just fed herself and the cubs a hot rabbit. She finishes the prowl and goes back to the cave.

She crawls up and around the dog-leg. The cubs are asleep now in a fur heap at the back of the tunnel. She pushes them with her nose for good measure, one grunts. She turns and turns, finding the right spot in the heap of leaves and dirt on the cave floor. She drops down, folds herself in, nose across tail, legs tucked under.

She is positioned between the cubs and the opening of the cave so the young are protected both from anything that might come in and also from their own unsupervised egress. Rabbit remains are scattered around the cave.

It is hot and moist in there, from all their bodies; it smells powerfully of animal.

The wolf lets out a long, forceful breath. She sleeps, satisfied, with only one eye slightly glinting, on guard for the possible though by no means inevitable return of her mate.

Just outside my front door, a cypridium, the wild orchid called a Lady's Slipper, has risen and holds its swollen purple globes barely above the melting snow.